GW01072149

Shadow Plays

Parthian
The Old Surgery
Napier Street
Cardigan
SA43 1ED
www.parthianbooks.com
www.shadow-plays.com

First published in 2010
© the authors 2010
All Rights Reserved

ISBN13 978-1906998-32-5

Editors: Megan Power
          Clare Scott
          Anthony Jones

Cover image by Stewart Dunwell
Cover design by Power, Scott, Jones, Jain
Typesetting by Megan Power www. meganpower.blogspot.com
Printed and bound by Dinefwr Press, Llandybïe, Wales

Published with the financial support of the Welsh Books Council

British Library Cataloguing in Publication Data

A cataloguing record for this book is available from the British
Library

To Robert,
Anthony Jones.

love Scott.

To Robert
Best wishes
annie Bell Davis

Shadow Plays

Edited by Scott Power Jones

PARTHIAN

CONTENTS

FOREWORD

Who among us hasn't tried to catch shadows? Be they ours or others, imaginary or too eerily real. Who hasn't been amused in making animal heads with hands and fingers on a bedroom wall: rabbit ears, an animal's dewlap, how vivid they seemed. Our own film noir. The unforgettable shadows we feared when young: the ghoul in the window, the clever shadow of a monster, his shoes always about to give the game away under the curtain. Child's play, sometimes endearing or, more often than not, menacing. And what of the shadows of dreams? The twenty-third Psalm also has a shadow in it, the shadow of the valley of death. And yet, isn't there a sun lurking somewhere, which makes the shadow possible? And where do shadows go afterwards? This was always something that concerned me when I was young - did they disappear into our bodies? Could shadows be our souls going for a walk?

In this fine collection of writings, the shadows are sometimes within: solemn phantoms, sinister faceless figures; death in the guise of the grim reaper. What binds these very different writers together (apart from being on the same writing journey), is Wallace Stevens' assertion that reality is the product of the most august imagination. Now reality can be hard work at times, and the imagination though embracing the world according to Einstein, can also be full of shadows. A writer lives in the shadow of the fear of failing both off and on the page, the terror of not finding the truth and the shadow which tells him or her that there is only a dead-end of total darkness.

There is much to admire in this anthology. The mordacity of love is cleverly delivered in such stories as "Chance Encounter - the Web" by Sarada Thompson; Megan Power's crafted story "The Steakhouse" also provides us with a chilling tale, all the more potent against a genial backdrop and jaunty dialogue. Annie Bell Davies, in "Free Fall", displays in limpid prose how one chance discovery can be a defining moment between two people. Here too, you will meet some strange beings; Helene James presents a comical approach with quick-witted dialogue in "Living with Wilfred"; Clare Scott in "Miss Margaret Jones" constructs a narrative which overturns our initial reading, defying its autobiographical tone.

Memoir and confabulation are also present in plenitude as the broad theme allows the writers to dip into early memories. Tracey Warr's fantastic bedroom encounters in "The Hole in the Wall" is deliciously evocative and enlivens the senses as does "Little Hands" by Rachel Coles, ethereal in its unpredictable rendering. Other pieces also delve into faraway places such as Singapore or take us on childhood adventures. There are memorable poems here too. The self-mocking tone of poems by Anthony Jones such as "Alcoholic's Lament" entangle with heartfelt love poems. In a similar vein, Niti Jain's timeless verse conveys a sense of loss and longing along with the duality of hope and despair. In reading "Saqqara Donkey" we identify with Amanda Miles's accomplished depiction of a creature's Sisyphean plight.

In this collection too we are fortunate in shedding light on the work of two Welsh language writers, Martina Davies and Sian Price. Mae gwaith Sian yn gyfuniad rhyfedd o dynerwch a dwyster fel a welir yn "Llefain y Lloer" ac fe gaiff ei gyfleu mewn ffordd ddramatig gyda'r lloer yn dyst i bob dim a ddigwydd. Yng ngwaith Martina hefyd, gwelir y ddawn o ddarlunio cymeriad gyda "Y Nos i Mi" yn goferu o ddichell a rhwystredigaeth. Hyfryd oedd eu cyhoeddi yma am y tro cyntaf. Nid rhyfedd ychwaith iddynt lwyddo i drosi eu gwaith i'r Saesneg gan ddangos mor ddeheuig ydynt ill dwy, yn y ddwy iaith.

This is once again a remarkable collection and in referring to one text by each writer, I hope to have highlighted the diversity of writings which can be found here. Perhaps the book itself from its inception was a reconstruction of Plato's Cave Allegory but that these writers managed to unfetter themselves from the shadows on walls and write towards the light. The title of the book, *Shadow Plays* also reminds one of the phrase, "May your shadow never grow less," a phrase of Eastern origin for those fleeing the devil: if he were to catch part or all of their shadows, they would then become first-rate magicians. Here, we witness writers who are developing their craft in becoming word-magicians with gusto.

I would like to thank all those involved in editing this book. This anthology marks the thirteenth year of the MA in Creative Writing at Trinity University. We are blessed at Trinity in having the dynamic internationally renowned publisher Parthian Books here on campus and Dominic Williams, their wonderful marketing director does far more than is required of him in making sure that all those involved learn how to produce a book worthy of their talent and the publisher's name. We are grateful to him for his expertise in helping to guide the work and broaden the horizons of those whose knowledge of the publishing field had until very recently been limited. Many writers who find themselves published for the first time in an anthology such as *Shadow Plays* will, I'm certain, go on to publish their own work in due course. As ever, I'd like to thank on behalf of the writers, the university and the Development Unit for their financial support; also, Kevin Matherick, whose enthusiasm in organising the Trinity Ffrinj Festival every year enables the writers to showcase their work in such prestigious places as the Dylan Thomas Boathouse and Halliwell; lastly, as always my thanks to Dr. Paul Wright, the wonderful Head of English for his invaluable encouragement and wisdom.

Finally, I must allow Jung to have the last word as it's difficult to let go of the meaning of "shadow" without thinking of his belief that "in spite of its function as a reservoir for human darkness - or perhaps because of this - the shadow is the seat of creativity."

MENNA ELFYN

Chance Encounter - The Web

Sarada Thompson

Approaching thirty, he was a dish to look at but desperately lonely as a long-term relationship had just ended. In the end he resorted to Internet dating. At the same time, she too recently bereaved, was looking for a mate. They clicked straight away, sharing many interests: food, wine, books, music and a fascination in arachnids, insects, the study of nature and the environment.

She invited him to meet for the first time at her house at the end of an isolated country lane. He was welcomed warmly and she lived up to more than his expectations. She was captivating, dazzling and had taken care to look beautiful. He was flattered and liked what he saw: her carefully kohl-lined eyes, sensuous, full, blood-red lips, figure-hugging black dress showing her hourglass figure and long, shapely net-stockinged legs in matching black stilettos.

It did not fail to impress. She had taken pains to prepare a sumptuous three-course dinner with red wine, all invitingly laid out with a single red rose in the middle of a beautiful laced tablecloth. His favourite music, Rachmaninov's Second Piano Concerto, was playing softly in the background, enhancing the romantic idyll. They dined, wined, danced cheek-to-cheek to the "Blue Danube" and thoroughly enjoyed each other's company before going to bed.

The bedroom was alluring, even theatrical, with silver glittering web-like patterns all over the walls and ceiling. He sank into a soft, red velvet bed of down and enjoyed a night of continuous, consummate passion which surpassed any that he had known before.

At dawn he became aware he was paralysed and could not flex a muscle; his very last consciousness was hearing her triumphant words on top of him, "You did say you like spiders, especially the Black Widow!"

An Alcoholic's Lament

Anthony Jones

When drunkenly I got back home to her
Pretending that I had not drunk at all
I could not hide my stumbling or my slur
Or tripping over dust balls in the hall.
I ran through the excuses well rehearsed
And promised yet again there'd be no more
Of wasted afternoons lining the purse
Of landlords who all viewed me as a bore.
I said I'd never drink again, again,
Do anything you wanted if you'd stay.
I know how drink has beaten many men
And driven us to terminal decay.
And now as I lie prostrate on the floor
I swear to you I'll not drink any more.

3

The Doodle Dangle Poem

Annie Bell-Davies

I've diddled and I've doodled
Since we cuddled and canoodled
I've lingered and I've dawdled
All day through

But now you make me dangle
My heart is in a mangle
And I'm getting in a tangle
Over you

First Signs of Spring

Clare Scott

Snowdrop and green leafblade have pierced the snow
To make a boxer's winning punched salute.
The spread of frost feathers are fading slow.
The fists of ice that seized and held the shoots
Release mountain springs, river water snakes
Explode silent across green-grey meadows.
Sprinkled with birds' chatter, the air awakes.
A breeze catches new smells before she throws
Them on to play with the sounds of full throat
Dancing calls, forming a rhythmic patter.
Girlchild Bridget, happy to stay remote,
Jumps and skips along the hopscotch ladder.
Serpent swans sail, their grace powered below
Movement and change make history show.

Storm

Sian Price

Blanced o ganhwyllau yn curo'r cysur,
Dawns ddiflas a dim electrig.
Salwch, sioc a siom.
Yn y tywyllwch trefnus.

Storm

Sian Price

Blanket of candles beats the comfort,
Dreary dance with no electric.
Seediness, shock, sabotage.
In the methodical darkness.

The Hole in the Wall

Tracey Warr

Eight o'clock bedtime always seemed so early. Even though I was a year older than my sister and five years older than my brother we all had to go to bed at the same time. In the summer the evening sunlight was still vivid through the filter of the bedroom curtains. And in the winter the streetlight shone into the room. I usually couldn't sleep for three or four hours after bedtime. I had a number of tactics for whiling away those hours.

I would listen to the furniture and the walls creaking and cracking as the house cooled down for the evening. I thought I could see tiny red monsters with square heads, making those cracking noises, as they climbed up the curtains like mountaineers. They weren't frightening monsters. I watched their antics, intrigued.

Sometimes I chatted and giggled with my sister,

Julie, and we tried to call to our little brother, Lee, through the wall into his bedroom next door. But Julie and Lee always got sleepy before me and after a while they ceased to answer. Or, if my mum came upstairs and heard us all talking, she would burst in and tell us off crossly: "Do you know what time it is? Be quiet and go to sleep!" If it was the second time in one night that we got caught whispering instead of sleeping then we could expect to have the bedclothes pulled back and each get a smack to go with the cross words.

I had a number of small torches secreted around the bedroom and I read under the bedclothes, steadily working my way through the entire children's section of the public library. But reading under the bedclothes was also a capital offence, eliciting smackings and confiscations and dire warnings about the future of my eyes.

If there was rain or a storm then I could entertain myself with that since my bed was next to the window. I would sit in my pyjamas on the leaking window sill, watching the thrilling displays of weather.

Or I could play the raspberry-window game which consisted of opening a small top window, hiding behind a curtain, and blowing loud raspberries out the window at bewildered passersby. Eventually the man up the road put a note to my mother through the letter-box and got me into a lot of trouble.

Some nights I listened to the muffled sound of the TV coming up through the floor with my dad's shouts of laughter joining the guffaws of the studio audiences. Or I could hear the tap, clack and whirr of my mum's comptometer in their bedroom as she laboured at the extra jobs she did to keep us all well looked after. I loved the satisfying noise of that machine and in the daytime she sometimes let me try it out.

Occasionally my sister would have a nightmare or wake up terrified and trapped at the wrong end of her tightly tucked in bed and I would have to jump to her assistance yelling, "It's alright! It's alright! I'm coming!" I would dig her out of the tangle of sheets and blankets and her smothered screaming and she would emerge with her damp hair clinging to her wet, red face. And sometimes she would talk in her sleep and I could amuse myself holding one-sided conversations with her that I knew she couldn't really hear. Or I had to be alert for the occasions when she would get out of bed, sleepwalking, and make for the door. I would have to head her off at the pass and gently coax her back into bed. Once she had me up and dressed in my school uniform before I realised that it was four a.m. and she was sleep-talking and sleepwalking.

Another time I woke abruptly to the thunder of her feet running across the room and the thud of her throwing herself on top of me.

But mostly there were long boring evenings when nothing happened and I had to tell myself stories in my head. I had a cast of recurring fantasy figures and narratives elaborated out of my reading or what I saw on TV.

And then I had the hole in the wall. It began as a slight dent or imperfection in the wall just above my bedhead where my dad and uncle had perhaps bumped the wall with furniture when we moved into the house. Little by little I tore away tiny shreds of rucked wallpaper and rubbed at the irregular edges of the dent. Flakes of plaster came away, falling into a small cairn down the back of my bedhead.

After many nights of absentminded fiddling it became a real hole. Tracing the edges and bowl of the hole was an unconscious twiddling I did just before falling asleep, akin to the way I wound a strand of my hair around and around my finger when I read. The hole was my version of counting sheep. It was my Bedtime Companion. Between awake and asleep, the stories I spun in my head seemed to be coming out of the hole in the wall, stirred out by my finger. Tracing the hole was the rhythmic accompaniment to the stories and my brother's soft snoring and the creaking climbing little red men on the curtains and the relentless fall of rain and the muffled TV laughter.

After two or three years I eventually cut through. The hole opened out into my brother's little box-room. Now we could put a finger right through and wiggle it around in greeting to Lee and his racing car duvet. My mum and dad had tutted and scolded as the hole slowly developed. Now they decided it was time to act. My dad knocked down the wall, and the hole. He replaced it with a brown wooden partition wall which gave my brother a bit more room (and us less). I watched the renovations innocently, as if the creation of the hole in the wall was somehow quite separate from me, merely a natural phenomenon.

When the work was finished the smooth brown face of the new wall gave no purchase for my twiddling finger. The night stories were imprisoned in its seamless surface.

Saqqara Donkey

Amanda Miles

Stillness of the night.
Full moon hanging in the sky
As desert winds kiss their promises amidst the stars.
Pyramids watched over by Hathor.
The donkey tiptoes on silent hooves
through the graveyard of the ancient kings,
with eyes that can see through your soul

Wedi'r Tywyllwch Daw Rhyddid

(Monolog Dramatig)

Sian Price

(Codir golau spot gwan ar wely ysbyty, mae pob dim yn wyn-yn glinigol iawn. Yn gorwedd yn y gwely gwelir menyw yn ei nawdegau, mae hi'n gorwedd fel ei bod hi wedi cael ei gwthio i waelod y gwely, mae hi'n gorwedd yno wedi crebachu fel baban yn y groth. O'i dwylo gwelir pibellau yn cysylltu â'r drip. Clywir sawl peiriant calon yn arafu a chyflymu. Wrth ymyl y gwely ceir cadair wen, mae hi'n wag-ceir rhan o'r monolog ei gyfeirio at y gadair. Mae hi'n siarad â neb, er fod yna deimlad o sgwrs)

Vera John *(acen cryf cymraeg)*

Ma' nhw'n gofyn cwestiynau twp fan hyn. "Have you opened your bowels today?" Rhyw ddoctor lliw oedd yma'n holi. Pobl ffein fyd chware' teg, er i mi fethu

After Dark Comes Freedom

(Dramatic Monologue)

Sian Price

(Spotlight up on a hospital bed. Everything is white, very clinical. We see an elderly woman lying in the bed. She is in her nineties. She is lying as if she has been pushed down the bed, she is lying like a baby in the womb. From her arms, tubes and drips are connected. In the background we hear the sound of a heart monitor. At the side of the bed there is a white chair. It is empty. Some of the monologue is addressed to the chair. She is talking to no one though it seems she is chatting to a companion.)

Vera John *(a strong Welsh accent)*

They ask silly questions here: "Have you opened your bowels today?" It was a coloured doctor that was asking. Lovely people. I have difficulty understanding them most of the time, but lovely. Nothing pleases me

15

deall nhw'n siarad weithiau. Er, does dim byd yn pleisio'n fwy na cael y nyrs Cymraeg yma yn tendio arnai.

Mae nhw'n dda yma, a dwi'n trial y ngorau i fod yn dda iddyn nhw hefyd. Trial peidio cwyno. "Vera fach," fydd hi'n dweud, a finne'n dair gwaith i hoedran hi. Wedi mynd yn fach gydag oedran chi'n gweld. Hen beth greulon, mynd yn hen. Dwi'n dal i fod yn ugain yn ym mhen. Yn dal i gerdded yn y sodlau gwych, yn dal i ddawnsio nes bod fy nhraed yn gwaedu, yn dal ifod yn berchen ar y byd.

(Mae peiriant calon yn sydyn yn cyflymu ac y mae hi'n gwegian mewn poen)

Newyddion oedd gan y doctor i mi heddi. *(at y gadair)* I chi'n gwybod yn hanes i? *(aros am ymateb ac yn cael dim)* Pa golled welai? A finne'n gaeth fel rhyw anifail i'r gwely yma. Dwi ddim yn un am gwyno, ond mae'r boen erbyn hyn yn...*(mae'n gwegian eto)* Dwi'n cadw'n brysur. Sudoku, mae'r hen ben yma'n dal i ddeall nymbers, anghofio enwau yn ddifrifol ond run peth fydd nymbyrs hyd nes fyddai'n...*(methu dweud 'marw')*.

Mae'n gallu bod yn reit dawel yma chi'n gwel'. Dim lot o gyfle i ddod i nabod rhein o'ch cwmpas - mewn a mas fyddwn ni erbyn hyn. Am le od i gwrdd â ffrind. Hen beth pleserus iawn mewn lle hynod o ddiflas. Dwi bob tro yn trial dod i nabod rhywun newydd, wedi trial bod y ffordd yna erioed. Dwi'n cofio'r athrawon mewn hyfforddiant yn dod aton ni i'r ysgol slawer dydd, rhai

more, though, than having the Welsh nurse tending me.

They are good here, and I try my best to be good to them as well. Try not to moan. "Vera fach," she calls me, even though I'm three times her age. I've shrunk with age, you see. Cruel thing, age. I'm still twenty up here *(pointing at her head)*. I'm still walking in those fabulous heels, still dancing until my feet bleed, I still own the world.

(The heart monitor increases in pace as she flinches in pain)

The doctor had some news for me. *(She turns to talk to the chair)* Do you know my fate? *(Waits for a reply, but has none)* What will I miss? I'm a caged animal in this bed. I'm not one for moaning, but the pain is...*(she flinches again)*. I try to keep myself busy. Sudoku. This old head still understands numbers. I forget names like there's no tomorrow, but numbers will be the same until I...*(can't bring herself to say "die")*.

It can get quite quiet here you see. You don't get much chance to get to know those around you. In and out they come. Strange place to meet a friend: a pleasure in a tiresome place. I always try to make friends, that's how I've tried to be all my life. I remember years ago, the training teachers coming in their flock to the school. Some of the other teachers would straighten their tails, ready to mark their territory, but I would try and make friends every time. Chatting away with the women, but trying to drag the men down to the hall on the weekends. *(Laugh)* I remember when Beryl came to

o'r athrawon eraill yn troi eu cefnau a'u cynffonau'n s tynnu'r dynion i lawr i'r neuadd ar y penwythnos am ddawns. *(chwerthin)* Dwi'n cofio'r tro pan ddaeth Beryl y ato ni gyntaf i ddysgu, a hithau'n cael y croeso sych gangweddill, ond mi oedd hi'n wahanol ac yn fodlon rhoi blas o'r triniaeth yn nôl a rhoi hwfft fawr i'r criw, gafael yn ym mraich i a chwerthin am eu pennâu. Dyna le bu cychwyn ein helyntion, am ddwy ddrygionus - hen baracs rhyfel oedd ein llety itha llym ond diawl os fyddai'r waliau yna'n gallu siarad. A dyna le i'r ddwy ohonon ni ddod ar draws Dai. Sssssht *(yn meddwl ei bod hi'n clywed y doctor yn dod)*

Mae'r doctor yna'n hwyr ar ei rownds prynhawn, finne'n meddwl i mi glywed e'n dod. *(mae hi'n gafael yn ei choes ac yn trial osgoi'r poen, mae'n siarad trwy'r boen)* Wedi bod yn y fyddin oedd Dai, wedi dod ato ni i ddysgu ar ôl gadael - wedi gweld hen bethau rhyfedd ond nid yn un i drafod hynna ag eraill. Dwi'n cofio dweud wrth iddo gyrraedd yn ei siwt wlân crand a'i satchel lledr brown "Dyma gariad i ti Ber."

Doedd e ddim yn hir cyn iddi ennill i gariad e chwaith - y tri ohonom yn bartners hyd y lle, y ddau bob tro yn sibrwd yn cynllunio rhyw gynllwyn i chwilio cariad i mi- methiant oedd pob cynllwyn. *(saib)* Yn driawd at y diwedd. Fe gollais i ddau ffrind o fewn hanner awr chi'n gwbo'. Fe ddaeth yr alwad i ddweud bod Beryl wedi cael trawiad ar y galon ac wedi mynd yn ddistaw yn yr ysbyty - doedd hi ddim yn hanner awr arall nes i'r ail alwad ddod i ddweud bod Dai wedi cael trawiad hefyd wrth ochr ei gwely hi - mae'n debyg o'r sioc. 'I

teach with us. She had the same welcome from the others but she was different, she gave as good as she got. Grabbed my arm and we trotted off, laughing.

That's when our shenanigans started, the mischief we got up to in those old barracks. If those walls could speak, as they say. And that's where we came across Dai. Ssshhhht *(she quiets down, thinking that the doctor is on his way)*

The doctor's late on his afternoon rounds. I thought I heard him. *(she grabs her leg but tries to ignore the pain)* He'd been in the army, Dai. Came to teach with us after he was released. He must have seen gruesome things there, but he was never one to talk about them. I remember him arriving in his woollen suit and his brown leather satchel. "There's a man for you Ber," I said.

And it wasn't long before she'd won his love. The three of us, partners. I could hear them whispering, plotting some blind date for me. But all the plotting was a failure. *(Pause)* A threesome till the end. I lost two friends within an hour, you know. The call came to say that Beryl had had a heart attack and died peacefully in the hospital. Half an hour hadn't gone by when the second phone call came to say that Dai had also died, at her bedside - they say - from the shock. His heart truly broken. I had to smile. From the moment they met, Dai wasn't far behind Beryl.

It was a hard day. *(Pause, changes the subject)*

galon wedi torri go iawn, roedd rhaid torri gwên - o'r funud i'r ddau gyfarfod roedd Dai ddim yn bell o le oedd Beryl a dyma fe wedi ei dilyn hi eto.

Diwrnod anodd iawn. *(saib, newid cyfeiriad)*

Fydd cinio ddim yn hir. Byta hefo'n ffroenau fyddai erbyn hyn, ac yn bachu arogl ar ginio'r rhai drws nesa'. Dwi'n torri'r syched yma hefo Ribena - am beth od i yfed a finne un tro wedi bod yn gaeth i te. Ar ol cinio fydd plant yn chwaer yn dod yma â hanes y pentre i mi. Chwarae teg. Dwi'n lwcus i gael pobl yn dod yma, ac yn gwerthfawrogi'r cwmni yn fwy nag erioed. Fydd rhaid dweud heno, y newyddion newydd sbon sydd gen i, colli'r hen goes sydd wedi bod yn ffrind reit dda i fi yw nhynged i nawr chi'n gwel'. Hen niwsens yw hi nawr-achos yr holl boen. Cael gwared arni hi fydd orau. I mi gael bod yn rhydd , i gael mynd ar galifant, i cael bod yn driawd eto.

Dinner won't be long now. I eat with my nostrils these days, steal a sniff from next door's lunch. I break my thirst with Ribena, of all things, having drunk so many cups of tea. After lunch, my niece and nephew will visit. They come with all the stories of the village. Fair play. I'm lucky to have them, and I appreciate the company. I'll have to tell them tonight, tell them my news. Losing this leg that's been a great friend to me. That's my fate. It's just a nuisance, and the cause of all the pain. Losing it is for the best. For me to be free, for me to go on an adventure again, for me to be a threesome again.

The Steakhouse

Megan Power

Those steakhouse girls were so clean. White shirts, white pants, white aprons. From the hostess to the barmaid it was like a local beauty pageant in there. Twenty-one-year-old creampuffs with smooth skin, shiny hair, straight teeth, happy natures. They had shoe habits, that's all, no needles or pipes involved. A few inhaled half a pre-performance joint but nothing harder.

Waitressing tips didn't cover rent, groceries, car payments, tuition and clothes so the girls jostled with each other and cajoled Saad, the Lebanese manager, for the dinner shift. Lunch wasn't too bad (noonsies) but what no one wanted was breakfast. Smelling of floor cleaner and burnt bacon, staffed with lardy horsefaces and disdainful queers, patronized by families and senior citizens, The Keg was like a completely different establishment at breakfast. No vim or vigor, just cooking.

But dinner was a study in seduction. Fresh flowers, mellow lighting, white tablecloths and black napkins, restless jazz. Despite the money and power that walked through the door, with their natty suits and platinum cards and connections, it was the harem that ran things, every section, every night: ponytails swinging, coconut body lotion wafting, mixing with the aroma of seared meat, lipgloss shining, laughter trilling. It was their show.

Committee meetings had gone over and the restaurant was jammed by the time he'd checked in at the hotel and made his way to the hostess station. A tall blonde dream seated him, set a menu on the table and reminded him to enjoy. He removed his coat and scarf and his server came along. Her loveliness nearly caused him to drool.

"How are we this evening?" she greeted him, leaning over to pour ice water into his glass.

"Hungry," he replied.

"Well we'll take care of that," she said, even her fake smile glorious.

He thought he'd seen her before, possibly on the arm of some conventioneer. She could have passed for a trophy wife with that confidence and grace.

After a basket of dense bread and The Keg's signature martini, she presented a serving tray of the house cuts, raw slabs perched on decorative lettuce in small pools of watery blood.

"All our beef is free range, grass-fed and butchered in-house," she said. "Personally selected by Chef Terrain, who comes to us from Qatar and the Seychelles, by way of Hong Kong."

In order not to ogle her, he stared at the meat.

With her free hand she pointed as she spoke. "This is the Tenderloin, our most popular cut. Here we have a dry-aged Prime Rib, a pepper rubbed New York Strip, a T-bone and finally, a melt-in-your-mouth nine ounce Filet Mignon which is marinated for a full twenty-four hours before it hits our infrared grill."

As he considered his options, girls passed the table with arms full of sizzling plates and bowls shooting steam. Finally he chose the Tenderloin with sides of Yukon Gold potato strings and sautéed chanterelle mushrooms and a glass of Fleur du Cap pinotage, at which point she remarked, "Excellent."

The red leather booths - maybe vinyl, he wasn't sure - were spaced for privacy, amenable to illicit proposals. The Keg was located on the second floor of the Grandview Shopping Center and attached to the high-rise Prince George hotel by a small skywalk. It was remarkably convenient, so much so he often wondered if it had been designed for the de facto purpose it served.

As he unwrapped his cutlery from the napkin and buttered a slice of sourdough bread, he thought of the old Orwellian saw, the key to a good steakhouse being knives. Here they were sharp enough to slit a wrist. He chewed the bread slowly, watched the girls' chaotic choreography and finished his martini.

When the steak arrived, he thought it looked obscene on a white plate devoid of garnish, the sides served in separate dishes plus a ramekin of creamy béarnaise, and in contemplating this he missed making successful eye contact while thanking her.

The contrast between the outer char and inner tenderness made him utter a soft grunt of pleasure, and he savoured the mineral flavour of the meat closest to the bone. The workday edge began to soften. He sipped his wine and leaned back in his chair.

"And how is everything here?" she breezed in, refilling his water glass.

"Delicious," he declared.

A short while later she asked if he had room for banana flan or a sampling of fine cheeses. He asked if he could have dessert delivered to his room. This was what was said.

"I'm sure we could," she said, holding his gaze, sizing him up. "Let me just check."

He hadn't expected the anticipation of those few minutes, possible rejection looming.

"Not a problem," she confirmed upon returning. She began clearing his plates and quietly asked, "Room number?"

He told her. Then with a nod she disappeared for a few minutes and came back with the bill.

"Here we go," she said, placing it to one side. "I'll take care of that for you when you're ready."

"And the...flan?"

"We'll have sent up."

"You...?"

"Uh huh."

"Perfect."

"It might take a little while."

"Oh, it's no rush."

She ran his card and returned it to him.

"Thank you very much. Enjoy your night."

"Thank you. I will."

And after that first time it always went the same. He killed time until her shift ended, taking the elevator to street level and walking to the corner of Argyle and Barrington, where the same homeless guy always loitered, shifting foot to foot in the cold. He handed over his doggie bag. The bum never spoke but gave a nod suggesting gratitude.

He walked a few more blocks to the harbourfront, admired the lit bridges and then walked back to the Prince George, where he went to his room and made a few calls. Looked at his notes for the morning. By then she'd clocked out, collected her gratuities, sweet-talked Saad and hurried across the skywalk to the elevator up to his room, knocking distinctively. While he caught the end of a game and finished a drink, she'd change out of her uniform, shower and make an entrance.

They were both drunk the night she died. He'd had too many scotches after a day of bad financial news and also she was late. He hadn't been sure she would come at all. When she finally knocked close to midnight he answered the door with an enormous rush of relief, and noticed that her smile was lopsided. Closing the restaurant had taken forever, she explained, dropping her purse on the floor. The girls were doing shots, helping the alcohol inventory along, and she'd done too many. She laughed and hiccupped. He smiled wanly. She went into the bathroom and he heard her stumble around before getting in the shower. He poured himself a drink and stood staring at the view of the McKay

Bridge over the harbour, realising how drunk he was.

Again he pondered the strange exhilaration of possible rejection. The few times she'd turned him down he'd wanted her more.

"We're actually out of our dessert menu tonight," she'd said sweetly. "Very popular. So sorry about that."

"When do you...get more?" he'd asked, unsure of the wording.

"Tomorrow. Definitely."

She'd never told him about the car accident over Christmas and the six weeks off work on account of the cast. No mention of how badly broken her leg had been.

But he was drunk and she was too and he didn't interpret her noise as pain when he pushed both legs all the way back behind her head. When she shuddered, he sped up. But he felt her body go slack, as though she'd fallen asleep, he stopped.

He said her name five times. Slapped her, testosterone coursing. Shook her. Tried all her pulse points. And nothing. He screamed and backed off the bed. Cursed and paced, fully erect. It would not go down. He tried to concentrate on breathing.

He collected himself and called the front desk.

"Someone has died in our room," he said.

The embolism ended it all. His career, her life. The Prince George hotel, The Keg steakhouse, the Commissioner's record, the city's bond rating, the public confidence.

At least he was still breathing, still walking around. Walking around was all he did nowadays. And sometimes as he wandered along the harbour, free of tourists and families in winter, he couldn't stop the clot image from forming in his mind, winding its slow death-bubble way up her leg to her heart. Destroying so much with so little force.

A Secret Game

Niti Jain

"Mommy, can I sleep with you? I don't like the maid," he sobbed.

"Go to your room," his mother said.

"She didn't listen did she? I told you it's our secret game. Don't tell her again. She doesn't love you. I do."

And she took off his clothes. She'd never know what else she took off.

Tick Tock

Amanda Miles

Lola had decided.

She would give him another ten minutes.

Earlier, Peter had offered to go out across the yard to the stables. To check on the horses after the storm. The storm that brought with it thunder and lightning as a prelude to snow.

The December afternoon had been oh so cold. Lola enjoyed a leisurely warm bath with her new floaty candles and aromatherapy oils. She dressed in her new toasty warm red flannelette pyjamas and matching dressing gown. The last thing she wanted to do was to leg it across a snow-covered yard to check on their hunters. So, when Peter kindly offered, she readily accepted.

Peter had shrugged himself into his old Barbour, pulled a thermal hat down over his ears, and climbed into his boots. As soon as he stepped into the moonlit night, he blended quickly with the shadows. The only way Lola knew he had reached the stables was when she saw the light coming on. Then, after a few minutes, it went off. She tried his mobile. It was switched off.

Ten more minutes.

She would gear herself up to facing the cold of the Boxing Day night.

Ten minutes came and went.

Bugger.

All sorts of thoughts were careering through her mind. He could have slipped and be lying on the floor unconscious. Perhaps one of the horses had kicked him in the head. What if he'd developed amnesia? Or maybe he'd disturbed a gang of horse thieves and was lying in a pool of bright red blood. What if an art dealer might have been lurking in the shadows, waiting for him to hand over one of the many pieces that had recently come into his possession? There were numerous possibilities. And now the ten minutes were up.

The time had come.

Reluctantly, but with a rising sense of panic, she tucked her new jim-jam bottoms into her boots, tied a scarf round her head, zipped up her old fleece jacket, grabbed the big torch and her mobile and went forth. Like a beacon into the cold night air.

The snow crunched and squeaked below her feet. For a minute she forgot her task and marvelled at the sparkly beauty of the snow glistening in the moonlight. Without thinking, the index finger on her right hand found the ring finger on her left and stroked the large diamond engagement ring that nestled against the band of gold.

A loud whinny and stamping of hooves brought her back to reality. Something was definitely up.

Lola managed the last few steps to the stable entrance on tiptoes.

The stable was in darkness.

She shone her torch around and saw her husband's coat thrown over one of the stable doors. Her hand jerked up to cover her mouth.

"Oh my God!" she thought. "They've stripped him and tied him up."

Then she heard a cough and, a few breaths later, some low chuckling.

She found the light switch and turned it on.

More low chuckling and a long "Ssshhhh".

"Peter! Are you there? Are you all right? What's happened? I've been worried sick…"

As she peered over the second stable door she felt the blood drain from her face right into the bottom of her boots. She steadied herself against the door and looked again.

There he was.

Buttock naked.

On top of Simon, the lad who helped with the horses. His hand was clamped over Simon's mouth.

"Jesus Christ! Peter …what's going on?"

Simon had struggled free from the hand.

"It's bleedin' obvious isn't it? We're shaggin'…that's what's going on!"

As Lola turned and ran she heard Peter telling Simon

to shut up along with several other instructions. She reached the house and slammed in through the front door. And locked it.

Peter was outside.

"Lola! Come on. I can explain."

Lola wasn't interested in his explanations. She gathered up some of his belongings, shoved them into a black bin bag (courtesy of the local council) and threw them out from the bedroom window.

"You'll hear from Alistair. Don't you contact him He's my solicitor. A week. That's what you've got to get your stuff or else it'll go in the cess pit."

The week had come and gone.

By prior arrangement, Peter had collected his things. The divorce had gone through at a pace. Alistair had seen her proud. Peter and Simon, who had been stable mates for some months apparently, had set up in a twee little flat in the next town.

She had heard Peter missed the horses.

Shame.

Lola was lonely though. She thought of her friends. The pairs of friends.

Then a magazine caught her eye.

It was the latest edition of *Horse and Hound*.

She flicked through the pages and looked at the classifieds. Two or four glasses of wine later she had penned an advert that she was emailing.

For a husband.

Definitely not a stable mate.

Y Nos i Mi

Martina Davies

Y nos i mi.
Daw'r nos yn ei hanterth
a'r sêr yn gôr
i lenwi'r tywyllwch
yn gynfas o drysor.

Wrth i'r dydd bellhau
daw'r tywyllwch a'i llynges
o greaduriaid man
i bori'n ei mynwes.

Y rhyfeddod gorau
yw pan fo'r nos yn dihuno.
Y barrug ar y ddaear
a'r blodau'n sïo

Daw'r nos a'i storm
yn arllwys ei gwychder
gan daflu'r goleuni yn wyn
yn ei thymer.

Safaf yn dawel
yn gwylio'r nos yn blodeuo.
Y dail a'r porfa,
y cyfan yn ailgydio

Arswydus, ofnus
Brawychus a chas.
Galwch e'n be chi moin,
Ond i fi,
Urddas yw enw'r nos.

Back to the Dark

Niti Jain

"You're leaving?" she spoke holding the tears back.

"I have to. This isn't working out."

"It was working out for the last 5 years. I ... I ..."

"Don't. I shouldn't have come."

She stared as he left. She found it. The metal felt cold. As she slit it, she felt nothing and then it was all dark.

Chasing Butterflies

Annie Bell-Davies

Rural Wales in the sixties was an innocent place to grow up.

It was a time when we had never seen black skin or an Indian takeaway and the sniff of an illegitimate pregnancy was the richest source of scandal a gossip's tongue could feast on.

TV was a treat reserved for tea time. Although we could only see our favourite show, Batman, if Dad returned from work in time to fashion an aerial from a broken matchstick and some wire stuck into the back of the TV. And we didn't have a phone in our house, let alone our pockets.

Childhood alliances came and went with the seasons but in the summer of 1967 my best friends were Eleri and Caroline and we spent most days walking in the hills around the village where we lived. Our favourite walk took us up over the hill at Cae-Glas fields to Bluebell wood. It wasn't far but the walk took us past the cemetery. We made it a rule never to talk as we went past the line of crooked stones but invariably one of us would imagine a sound that would send us screaming and running beyond death's reach. Then Caroline would regale us with the story of the woman in grey, the only ghost story she knew, and we would hold hands and walk a little faster until the perceived danger was gone.

If we had been older, we might have stopped to look at the estuary as it twisted its way to the sea or at the tide as it heaved its way in and out like breath. But we were seven and even the castle on the distant hill held no interest. It was just a castle, after all, and we'd seen it every day of our lives.

We had played in the woods for weeks that spring; as the bluebells came and went, but as summer took its turn, we stayed at the top of the field and played in the sunshine that teased out the freckles on my nose.

"Let's play rounders," Caroline said that day, in her usual authoritative tone.

We haven't got a bat or ball, was my only objection.

"Well we can throw a stone instead."

"As long as you don't throw it at me, Caroline Walters," Eleri glared at her suspiciously. It would not be beyond belief for Caroline to do something spiteful if the mood took her and the future policewoman, Eleri Evans, knew it.

"Why don't we play tag then," I offered and soon we were inventing the rules of tag-rounders.

But it wasn't long before Eleri's voice, challenging us with a you can't do that, sent Caroline into a seven year old huff – and there is no age that can accomplish that better and there was never a girl who could carry it off with more alacrity than Caroline Walters.

Sensing trouble, I thought quickly.

"Let's make daisy chains," I suggested.

Caroline flopped to the ground in instant agreement, the skirt of her dress billowing around her like a crinoline as she began laying claim to all the perfect daisies. Eleri hovered for a moment; her wiry frame, perfect for running, meant she liked the games where she was chased best. But seeing Caroline and me so intent in our endeavours, she sank to her knees with a sigh and stoically threw herself into the task of killing daisies for art.

"I can plait hair," Caroline announced after a while. Her air of superiority honed, even at that age, like a needle that could get under my skin and irritate.

"No you can't," Eleri protested. Like me, she recognised the bully in Caroline but where I stroked the ego and appeased the temper, Eleri challenged.

"Oh, yes I can."

"But even Mandy can't do plaits and she's nine."
Eleri was firm.

If she had been standing, Caroline would have stamped her foot; she was always stamping her foot when she heard something she didn't like. Instead, she glared at Eleri before abruptly rising to her feet and I watched as the perfect daisies fell forgotten to the floor and were trampled beneath a polished Start-rite sandal.

"I'll show you!"

Without warning my hair was pulled from the tidy

ponytail my mother had arranged and the first fist of nervousness lodged in my stomach.

"Stop it," I protested, although it came out more like a whine and I saw the flash of pleasure in the forget-me-not eyes.

"Don't be such a baby. I'm not going to hurt you," Caroline scolded and I sat with tears prickling my eyes, as she grabbed and twisted my heavy curls.

Eleri watched. "You're doing it wrong," she said at last and tried to take control.

Like a rag doll, I was pulled by one then the other, until I screamed the high pitched scream of seven and they both stopped.

"Let go," I demanded and pushed them both away. Fighting tears, I sniffed and raised my hand to my head, frantically trying to smooth out the knots that their fingers had tangled into my hair.

"Sorry Jen," Eleri muttered as she stood, contrite, her eyes swimming in watery guilt.

"Don't say sorry. She's just a big baby." Caroline glared from me to Eleri and as she moved her hair swished perfectly across her shoulders. It was straight and gold as a daffodil. How I envied that hair. My own was thick and wild; the colour of the pots my Nana used for planting Bizzy Lizzies. My mother cursed it daily as she struggled to tame it and cage it in elastic.

"Look she's crying," Caroline needled, poking my arm in ridicule. Knowing that the gleam of satisfaction would not be removed easily from her eyes, I ran away from them.

I had barely disappeared over the crest of the hill

before my foolishness struck me, but I was too proud to go back even when I heard Eleri call me. Besides, now that I was away from them, I had no reason to stop my tears and my shoulders shuddered as I sobbed. My tummy hurt from nervous knots and with my arms folded tight against my ribs, I started blindly for home.

It wasn't until I had passed Cae-Glas fields that I made any attempt to retie my hair. It was more than I could manage and I knew that I was heading for a row when I got in for messing it up.

Rows from my mother were normal. Well, I say normal. They were horrible and twisted me up inside like rope, but they happened a lot. I could never have articulated the foreboding that prickled at my neck and my palms whenever I entered the kitchen in the certain knowledge that I had displeased her again but I felt it. I felt it deeply.

Alan, my brother, didn't have rows. He was three years older and although I'd like to say he had learned to be good, I believe his nature had simply made him that way. Alan was never moved to chase a butterfly (that would lead him to fall into a puddle), or practice roly-polys, when he found the perfect patch of grass (that would stain his clean clothes green). Alan was a "good boy". Alan was Mammy's "good boy".

I never resented his goodness, but sometimes, when my mother's eyes sought mine to accuse and chastise, I envied it a little.

As I started the walk down to the village, the horror of what I had done struck me like a lightning bolt. Having left my friends behind, I would have to walk past the cemetery on my own and my heart started to pound in my chest.

The cemetery scared me. Death scared me. Even the thought that Grandad was there and would do me no harm did not soothe me. I stopped walking, biting my lip and sniffing loudly as I contemplated my dilemma. Below me to the right was the village; it was just a field away, close enough to reach in minutes but I had never walked that way before. It looked easy and infinitely more appealing than the tombstones that loomed before me.

I crossed the gate and was halfway down the field before I knew it. It was easy and as I got closer to the bottom of the field, it looked like I would come out near Nana's house. A great idea struck me; Nana would bring my hair back under control and Mammy need never know that I had messed it up and walked home alone. I might even get something nice to eat if Nana had been baking. My spirits soared.

But a few steps from victory, disaster struck. The feet that had been confidently striding towards my goal, found softer ground and I felt runny mud ooze over the rim of my shoe and into my sock. Panic seized me. I tried to yank my foot out but the movement and the fact that another step found the same slippery goo sent me tumbling backwards. I was sitting in a bath of cold, sticky mud. I got up quickly, hoping the mud had not had time to ruin me but I felt it heavy in my knickers, like poo, and I sobbed aloud. I was in so much trouble. Nothing could save me now and the knots in my tummy twisted so tight it squeezed hot pee down my legs.

Blindly, I pushed through a gap in the hedge and although I knew it was wrong, I went through an unfamiliar gate and walked around a house until I was on Nana's street. Even Nana could not fix this mess and with resigned trepidation, I wandered solemnly home.

Mammy was in the kitchen, standing at the sink gutting fish, their shiny entrails piled on old newspaper at her side. Her smile faded as soon as she saw me and I started to cry.

"I'm sorry," I blubbed, as my mother took in the full horror of my appearance.

When I looked in her eyes, I wanted her to see past the mud. I needed tenderness and love but she saw the ruined clothes, the laundry she would have to do, the shoes that had cost so much and all I saw was weary frustration and rage.

In the middle of the kitchen I was unceremoniously stripped and roughly washed. Then, without warning, I felt the sting of her palm on the soft flesh of my backside. She smacked me maybe five times as I pleaded with her to stop and then howled when, from the corner of my eye, I saw Alan watching.

"Don't let him see," I cried between sobs but my mouth was distorted and wet and the words were incoherent.

When she finished, pyjamas were found and forced around my quivering body. My eyes sought Alan's, pleading silently for a crumb of sympathy but, ashamed, he lowered his pink-cheeked face.

There was no snack, no glass of milk to comfort me as I was marched upstairs. Even Felix was shooed roughly from his place on my bed. I curled up by my pillow feeling desolate. Tears bubbled from my eyes and I wiped the snot from my nose with my sleeve. And then a new fear grabbed me. What if he was cross with me too? My mother's anger was one thing but Dad's would have broken me and I waited nervously for the sound of his homecoming.

Then I heard the train and felt the familiar tremble as it rumbled slowly past our house and I lay perfectly still, straining my ears to hear the sound of his key in the lock.

As his cheery hello called to us, I covered my ears against the noise of her voice telling him of my wickedness and worse, the words that I knew would come from her mouth, "I wish she was more like Alan. We never had this trouble with him."

His voice came then, calm and firm; soothing her and moments later I heard the welcome creak on the stair.

I forgot my throbbing bum and sat up, wiping away my tears. I wanted to be his brave little girl, strong like him but as the door opened and his eyes met mine, I dissolved.

"Daddy," I wailed. "She smacked me."

He didn't say anything. He simply sat on the end of my bed and opened his arms and I threw myself against him. I knew exactly the place on his shoulder where my cheek fitted and I rested there, gulping for air as the smell of pipe tobacco and Old Spice calmed me more than lavender or chamomile ever would.

"You've ruined your school shoes," he said at last, but from his mouth the words were gentle.

"Caroline pulled my hair," I began with a hiccup and soon I had told him all about the cemetery and the muddy alternative. I even told him about Alan watching as Mammy had smacked me until I felt raw. I trusted my words to him, knowing he would know what to do with them.

He cuddled me for a minute after I had finished, whispering that everything would be alright before making me promise that I would never go walking alone again.

"Now are you ready to say sorry to Mammy for ruining your shoes?" he asked and I nodded against his shoulder.

His hand came up then and he stroked my hair and kissed my forehead. "Come on then," he said. "And then we'll see if we can get Batman."

With my hand in his, I stood before my mother and said sorry for getting so muddy.

Her lips remained tight but she nodded and haltingly reached out and ruffled my fringe.

"Be more careful in the future," she told me, but the sting had gone from her voice and I knew that forgiveness would come, like sunshine after thunder.

Later that night, after he had read me a story and tucked me in, their voices rose up to me in the dark. I couldn't make out the words to start with but as their volume rose I heard my name. She was saying that I needed to learn something but the something was lost on the stairs. More words came; muffled and incomprehensible and then his voice, loud:

"Don't you ever smack her again. And that's final."

My heart soared. There is nothing more secure, more comforting than hearing someone with authority stick up for you and despite his sweeter nature, he was always the real authority in our home. And safe in the knowledge that he, above all others, loved me, I fell asleep.

Mammy didn't smack me again, although I probably provoked her more than once because I never could stop chasing butterflies or turning roly-polys.

A Horse Story

Hélène James

I recognised the horse immediately. Call him white, but of course he wasn't white at all, just not brown or black. A kind of beige, buff, the colour of mushroom. When the sun brushed his back, his matted coat blended with the scorched grass of the season. Bits of dry mud hung from his underside and along his legs. As it had not rained for some time, he'd been at work with little time for grooming.

He was led by a young man with dark shoulder-length hair, wearing a T-shirt with a faded motif on the back and cream coloured shorts. On his feet were sandals that had trod the dusty paths of many tourist seasons.

The first time I saw the horse, he was behind a garden fence leaning into the road. He stood there, gazing ahead with eyes submerged in sorrow at his narrow space. I'd seen him in other places too; the same doleful gaze that pleaded for the friendship of his own somewhere in the shade of pine and olive trees.

With crates of coke and beer strapped to his back, he rode on his hips, the weight pressing into his hinds as he trudged up and down the cobbled steps, the breeze dispensing his musty smell. Passing tourists watched and photographed the quaint custom of the land, some pitying the animal with little thought to the refreshments they had just consumed.

Much like complaining about the environment while dumping waste, changing landscapes, answering the mobile or just leaving the lights on without the gift of solar.

Gower

Megan Power

If we were still together
I'd take you out to Gower
Wander over limestone cliffs
Until the golden hour

And as the tide came in
Sun consumed by sea
We would saunter back
To a small white B&B

Drift about the room
Til our bodies meet in
Crescent-shapes like Rhossili Bay's
Curving, placid beach

But we are not together
To my static regret
And like that trip to Gower
It's something I can't forget

Dim Ond Tywyllwch

(Monolog Dramatig)

Martina Davies

'Dim ond ddoe weles i e. Yn cerdded lawr y stryd, 'i lyged e fel dwy ogof dywyll, gwag. Dim byd i weld ond corff yn symud i guriad amser...symud fel nodyn ar bapur...'i fywyd yn datod o flaen 'i lyged. Gymres i'r cam cynta 'na tuag ato, rhyw obaith anweladwy yn corddi tu fiwn i fi. Odd raid i fi siarad ag e, clywed 'i lais annwyl unwaith 'to. Clywed e'n gweud wrtha i y bydde popeth yn iawn...bo' ddim ishe fi boeni rhagor achos bydde fe na i fi. Trwy ddŵr a thân, na be' wedodd e...dŵr a blydi thân. A finne mor naïf, yn credu'r cwbl fel oen bach swci.

Bob bore dwi gorfod dihuno yn y gwely gwag ma. Teimlo'r fatras oer o dan 'y 'nghorff i. A fi'n gorwedd fel babi bach yn 'i gwrcwd. Agor llyged i wagle mawr. Blasu surdeb y nôs yn fy nghêg. Gorwedd yn gorff

Only Darkness

(Dramatic Monologue)

Martina Davies

It was only yesterday when I saw him walking down
the street, his eyes like two dark, empty crevices. An
empty body moving to the pulse of time...moving like
a note on paper...his life unwinding before his eyes. I
took that first step towards him, an invisible hope
brewing inside me. I had to speak to him, hear his sweet
voice once again. Hear him say that everything would
be OK...that I don't have to worry because he will be
there for me...no matter what...that's what he said...and
me, so naïve, believing every word like a little child.

Every morning I have to wake up in this empty bed.
Feel the cold mattress under me while I lie like a baby.
Open my eyes to a big empty space. Taste the night's
sourness in my mouth. A wounded body lying on the

glwyfus ar y gwely gwâg. Arogli ei arogl e yn ddwfwn yn y 'pilws' melyn a gobeitho gweld 'i wyneb yn troi i edrych arna'i...saib...ond y cyfan dwi'n 'i weld yw cysgod corff yn gorwedd ar y fatras oer. Dim cnawd i fi gael gafel ynddo'n dynn...teimlo gwres 'i gorff e'n lledu dros fy nghorff i yn oerni'r bore...saib...se ni ond wedi gwued rhywbeth...trial...na ble odd e, reit o'n flaen i...ac am eiliad, un eiliad fach weles i gysgod dros'i wyneb e. Cysgod y person oedd arfer bod. Ro'dd e'n cydnabod bo' fi 'na, eisiau gwued rhywbeth? Dwi'n siwr...ishe gwued sori...gweles i'r ysfa yn 'i lyged e...o'dd rhywbeth yn 'i dynnu fe atai, yr ysfa 'na am gariad a'n tynnodd at ein gilydd yn y lle cynta.

A na phryd ddath hi, y bitsh fach brwnt...cydio'n dyn yn 'i fraich e. Welodd hi fi...yr hen ast...twlodd hi un lwc fygythiol atai...a'i gwallt coch fel tân yn llosgi'r aer gan adael arogl càs ar 'i hol.bitsh...odd i llyged hi'n trial torri twll yn yn ben i...*Cadw draw*...na beth odd hi'n gwued wrthai, *So ti'n haeddu fe*...wedyn bant a hi...carlamu i ganol y bwrlwm...a fe'n 'i dilyn hi'n addfwyn.

O ni'n wag...ddim yn gwbo' beth i neud...sefyll ar gornel stryd yn fud yn gweld e'n cwmpo trw' mysedd i fel tywod man...weles i'r wên fach roiodd e i fi...cyn iddi hi ddod. Yna'r wên obeithiol honno'n diflannu... fel tân ar fatsien yn llosgi cyn marw mas. Un garreg fach o obaith wedi'i daflu i ganol yr ogof cyn suddo i'r llonyddwch unweth 'to. Gan adael fi ar gornel stryd fel crwydryn unig.

cold mattress. No flesh for me to hold onto tight. Feel the warmth of his body spreading over my body in the morning's chill...(*pause*)...if only I had said something...try...there he was, right in front of me...and for a second, one little second, I saw a shadow over his face, a glimpse of the person he used to be. He acknowledged that I was there, he wanted to say something, apologise, I'm sure...I saw the madness in his eyes...something was pulling him towards me, the madness for love that threw us together in the first place.

And that's when she came, the bitch, grasping his arm tight...(*pause*)...she saw me, she threw one dirty look my way...her red hair burning the air around her...her eyes burning a hole in my head. *Stay away*, she was saying, *You don't deserve him!* And away she went...galloping to the middle of the crowd and him following her like a lamb.

I was empty...I didn't know what to do, standing on the corner of the street mute, seeing him fall through my hands like fine sand. I saw the little smile he gave me...before she came, then the same hopeful smile fading away.

There's nothing left of him any more...nothing...only old cups sitting on the wooden table next to the bed ...the dried ring from his coffee cup looking at me ...reminding me of what used to be. I can't feel anything, only the dryness in my mouth. My lips are

Does dim ar ôl ohono rhagor...dim...dim ond hen gwpanau gwag ar y ddesg bren ar bwys y gwely...y staen coffi 'di sychu'n grychau ar 'i hochr. Sai'n teimlo dim chwaith. Dim ond y sychder yn fy ngheg. Ma' ngwefusau'n dyn fel lastig sych yn barod i rwygo'nwaedlyd. Dim ond cusan sy' ishe arna i. Un cusan fach wrth y gwefusau llawn i roi'r lliw nôl yn fy rhai i. Ond does dim cusan ar gyfyl y lle. Dim ond fi...yn gorwedd yn ddiymadferth ar y gwely fel cleren yn sownd mewn gwe corryn.

Mae'r boen yn mynd yn ormod. Alla i ddim 'i dioddef e rhagor...ma'r gwaed yn pallu llifo a'r cleishe piws yn gwaethygu...yn llyged i'n suddo'n ddwfnach i'r sgerbwd sy' mor barod i roi miwn dan y pwyse. Ma'r galon hon 'di torri...a does dim allai neud amdano rhagor...un crefas dwfwn 'di hollti'r glustog goch, gynnes miwn manhyn...yn gwaedu'n dawel bach. Shwt all un person achosi shwt gwmint o ddiodde? Rhwygo bywyd yn ddarne man a chau'r drws yn glep ar 'i ôl...heb hyd yn oed edrych nôl. Cerdded mas heb oedi...yn ddiedifar...dideimlad.

hard like a dry elastic band, ready to bleed with each crack. One kiss, that's all I ask for, one sweet kiss from those warm lips to put colour back into mine. But there's no kiss in sight. Only me...lying helpless on the bed like a fly stuck in a spider's web.

The pain is too much, I can't cope anymore...the blood is slowly receding and the purple bruises getting bigger by the day. My eyes are retreating into the skull, the tip of the iceberg, which is about to give away under the pressure. This heart is broken, and there's nothing I can do about it; one deep crack in my soul...bleeding quietly. How can one person cause so much pain? Rip my life to shreds and close the door behind him ...without looking back. Walk out without feeling, without regret...

Childhood Memories - Trapped

Sarada Thompson

My memories of childhood are idyllic, as I was born in Singapore, which is on the equator, blessed with sunshine and greenery all throughout the year. The happiest memories were by the seaside bathing in hot-warm waters, picking seashells and seaweed usually to adorn my grand, elaborate sandcastles.

One memory is etched firmly in my experience, not quite so idyllic. My father and his brothers, being in the Civil Service, were entitled to rent holiday bungalows by the sea. One December we all met in one such old colonial building in a remote part of Changi. All the aunts, uncles and cousins arrived and we had an expansive room each with basic en-suite and an adjoining smaller bedroom for the children.

It was an old timber house raised from the ground, enabling cars to be parked below. Set back from the seafront, we had a little walk up to the edge where there were some steep stone steps which dropped down to the beach. When the tide came in, it served as a breaker and we could hear the waves thumping from the house.

It was a full moon that night and we were all excited, especially the youngsters, as we were all together. The mothers between them were preparing meals and the men were busy, pleasantly arguing about setting the world right and general current affairs. We children gathered to amuse ourselves into a natural group under the supervision of the teenagers. It promised to be a great holiday season, and we were so energised we could not go to sleep.

It was late into the night when I heard moans from the room where my Aunt Lakshmi and family were. The third cousin, Kanan, was always a little odd, quite unlike his brother Shiva and sister, Shantha, who shared many childhood chats and play. We could hear the moans become groans and then Kanan called out, "Can you not see the torches?" At that moment I thought I did see torchlights!

And then through the timber walls we heard the plaintive cries from the youngest cousin, "Can you not hear the clanging of chains? They are crying out, awful cries to release them. They are in pain, awful pain!" My brother and I climbed into our parents' bed for comfort where we all huddled together until we fell asleep.

The next morning we were told by the adults that little Kanan was prone to nightmares, and he had difficulty settling into the new holiday surroundings.

Aunt Sita suggested a walk for all of us. It was greeted with enthusiasm and we took a walk along a winding coastal path set a little way off the edge with a deep drop to the sea. As we were enjoying the refreshing sea breeze in the relatively cool morning, it was Kanan who stopped and pointed to an isolated tree and said, quivering, "What's that?"

We followed his pointed finger to gnarled frangipani tree and could not see anything. He then said, "It's got blood caked up and oozing and there are chains around him and he is beckoning us!"

It was Aunt Sita who snapped at us to turn around, threw a cardigan around the little boy and marched us all back to the house.

I cannot remember much about our short stay there. We were told Kanan had been taken ill and was feverish. Our holiday was shortened and we returned earlier than anticipated. Despite the adults telling us Kanan was subject to nightmares and very sickly, we found out he not only became very ill but had all sorts of alternative treatments and, we much later learned, some form of exorcism. He did eventually recover completely.

We heard later that the house was once an old Japanese concentration camp and British soldiers were tortured and trapped in the premises. For me that holiday was a memory which left me with even more questions than answers.

Night Time

Anthony Jones

I lie in the darkness
Naked and unslaked
My body, melting, sweltering
In the cool blue crystal liquid glow
Of the night time radio.

Your softly-spoken snoring
Gnaws away adoringly
Into my fatigue,
Your every exhalation
A cooling consolation on my back.

A Promise to a Better Morning

Niti Jain

sleep evades
dreams desert
the night is long
the dawn far away

sleepless eternity
descends once more
a crescendo of noises
and yet all silent

the shadows of the dark
the music of the silence
the night prolongs
into a tussle

tussle between
a vacant voice
a seamless dream
and a promise

a promise to a better morning.

Living with Wilfred

Hélène James

Edna Bright blew out the candle by her bedside, drew the damp bedclothes around her shoulders and snored her way into a deep dream. She was back at the farm. Two removal men were loading a van with boxes of clothes she had never seen, ignoring her own possessions. The boxes were hatching like Russian dolls and the lads looked at her in despair.

"Grandma, you should have ordered a larger van," one said before they climbed into their seats and drove off.

"What about my furniture?" she called after them. "My bed? Table and chairs," but her voice didn't come.

"That's right," Maud said, coming from behind. "You shouldn't have dumped my things."

Edna turned to face her sister. Her skin was pale and

her hair, unbraided, lay loosely around her shoulders. She was wearing the same flowered dress she wore when she died.

"What's your game, little sister? What do you want?" Edna asked unperturbed, extending a hand towards her.

"You thought you could dump my stuff, didn't you? Well, I hid most of it!" Maud laughed the sound of a trumpet, then twirled round and dissolved through the air.

The cacophony intensified with each burst of laughter, throwing Edna awake. "That's odd," her eyes sprang open, leaving the dream behind. "Where's the music coming from? I'm sure I never left the radio on."

She lit the candle, pulled a quilted dressing-gown over her long flannel nightdress and stepped into a pair of fur-lined slippers. The noise from below stopped.

It had been a long day. The removal men had called early; surprised at how little she was taking, loaded up and delivered to her new home in Forsham by mid-morning.

When Maud died, the reality of her spending hit Edna hard; unpaid credit cards were witness to the rails of unworn clothes, stacks of shoes and knickknacks that their meagre pension could ill afford. She had no option, selling the farm was the only way.

Finding Gorse Cottage didn't take long. A property in a nearby village had been empty for some time and they were practically giving it away. "Just as well, because it was all I could afford," Edna sighed, snuggling back into bed.

After living on a farm all her life, it felt strange to be in a little cottage that lacked the comforts and familiarity of her childhood home. She missed the dogs especially. When it became difficult to get farmhands, both Maud and she decided it was time to let the stock go, first the cows, then the sheep. Only the dogs stayed. Freddie outlived his beloved mistress by a few weeks, Jessie followed her mate within days.

Edna began to drift back into sleep, when the trumpet set off again, this time in short bursts of staccato notes at a higher pitch. "Oh, bother!" she snapped, walking across the bare floorboards, then carefully taking each creaky step downstairs. "Another thing to sort out," she noted.

As she reached the last step, the noise stopped.

"Well, I'm damned. Now I'm imagining things," she exclaimed, as the candle flickered a few times and went out.

Gorse Cottage was close to the edge of the woods, not far from a river. There were no street lights. The last owners had apparently removed all bulbs and she hadn't had a chance to replace them. Somewhere in the room was an armchair, she felt her way around till she found it and sat down. The muscles in her arms still ached from washing down the walls and scrubbing the wooden floors. There was no time to unpack all her belongings, the radio could be anywhere. She leaned back in the seat not knowing what else to do when she became aware of a peculiar smell. "Phew, what's this?" she sniffed, as something wafted past her and with it, the odour drifted away.

She was tired. The luminous hands of the clock showed twelve; she had slept no more than two hours. Her eyelids felt the weight of recent events and closed.

Earlier in the day she had walked two miles to the village shop. The store, in the centre of a square, was a hodgepodge of old and new, with low ceilings and traditional black and red tiled floors. The fixtures and fittings were recent and the shelves well stacked. Along the far end were a display fridge with fresh meat and a counter with a range of cheeses. Two women were engaged in local gossip and a small boy was rearranging a row of tinned soup. The owner, shaped like an oversized egg with a waistband looking for somewhere to cling, glanced up.

"You're the new owner of Gorse Cottage, I take it," he said in a voice that didn't seem to come from him. He folded his arms across his chest and leant back against the counter. "It's been some time since anyone has occupied it."

Edna thought she detected a little titter, but when she searched his face, it was passive. He was a man somewhere in his fifties, with hair sculptured into a piece of abstract art. His eyes were small, narrow, lost in the facial growth of the last few days. A number of grooves, like horizontal trenches, were ploughed into his forehead and until he spoke, made him look like the devil himself.

"Bob Smith is my name," he carried on. "Trust you'll find everything you need here."

The two women at the back of the store stopped their chatter and stared without shame. The small boy dropped a can of soup on his foot and yelled out.

"One lamb chop, a tomato, one onion and two mushrooms, please," Edna said, undeterred. "That's all. I prefer to shop as I need. Gets me out of the house," she added, challenging the women's stares. Whatever their problem, they're not intimidating me, she thought as she placed her shopping into a bag and left the store.

The walk along the main road was arduous with a constant stream of traffic driving through puddles of recent rain and forcing Edna into the grass verge. She'd have to find an easier way, try a shortcut through the woods, she thought. When she got back, she looked at the estate agent's map and drew a triangle around Forsham. The path along the bank and through the woods was considerably shorter and cut out the road.

Sleep wouldn't come the second time and the fusty air of the unlived-in dwelling lingered. Edna looked out of the window across fields, beyond her garden. The sun had begun its journey and the sky had an array of colours that promised a good day. The silhouettes of trees had come alive with twittering birds. "I suppose I'll get used to it," she sighed. "They say time heals. Do I have enough time left?"

She wandered into the kitchen and arranged a cup, saucer and jug of milk on a tray. While the kettle boiled, she placed two teaspoons of loose tea into a teapot, one for the pot and one for herself, then poured in the water and carried the tray into the living room. As she sat down, there was a knock outside.

"Now, who can that be at this hour?" she asked herself, shuffling to the door.

For a small cottage, the door was wide, set in a heavy frame and Edna yanked it with the full force of her farm hand. She remembered the estate agent promising to grease the hinges before she moved in, but once the sale was made she never saw him again.

There was no one at the door.

"Dammit! I did hear something, I'm not going batty," she muttered to herself and with a determination to find out, stepped into a pair of Wellingtons and walked round the back of the house.

The garden was testimony to the general neglect. The lawns looked like they hadn't been cut for years, with nettles suffocating a number of struggling trees. Along the border, wild roses with few leaves and buds that never came to flower clung hopelessly to a collapsed fence. "Anyone there?" she called out, looking in all directions. In the nearby woods, an owl answered and the air hushed again.

The tea had gone cold. Edna picked up the cup, idly considering making another, when something knocked her elbow and the liquid tipped into her lap. She stood up quickly, letting it trickle onto the floor, then replaced the cup on the tray. The stench she had become aware of earlier was back. There's someone here, she thought, as an alarm ran through her body.

She stopped her breath and listened. There was an eerie silence that momentarily raised the hairs on the back of her neck. She released her breath, then held it back again and waited. She knew that if she showed any sign of fear she'd be beaten. As a little girl, one of their farm dogs once went for her. "Look him in the eye,

Edna, look straight at him," her father called out. "Show him you're not afraid, make him understand you are his friend." Later, he placed her on his lap and explained. "He challenged you out of his own fear. He chased you because he was afraid of something so small."

Edna raised her five foot another inch and heightened her senses. The air was stale, without movement. Something rotten, neither dead nor alive, was about.

In the morning light she noticed changes in the room. The boxes left by the men along one side of the wall were now stacked by the door. One of the chairs was knocked over and no, she did not trip over anything in the dark. She went over the events of the previous day, slowly recalling every incident since she moved in and suddenly she had the notion that she knew.

"Wilfred?" she asked in a voice she had used when admonishing the dogs.

"How do you know my name?" came a gruff answer, but when she looked around, she saw no one.

"Not telling," she answered, chuffed that she had guessed right.

While clearing the cobwebs amid cracked plaster of the mottle and daub walls, she noticed the name Wilfred carved into one of the old beams. It was like a child's hand, awkward, with irregular, but deeply grooved letters. "I wonder how old the cottage is," she considered. "Never thought to ask."

"So that's why the sniggers, the unusual interest,"

she surmised. When leaving the village shop, she thought she heard Bob Smith pick up the phone and say, "Looks tough as old boots, we'll see how long this one will last," but dismissed it.

As she was considering the best way to deal with the situation, her hand jerked again and the cup went over, this time spilling onto the floor.

"So that's your idea of a practical joke?" Edna said, undaunted. "Look, if you stop knocking over my tea, I'll make you one. How about it?" she said, screwing her eyes up and searching the room. In the far corner stood an old gent with long tousled grey hair, a thin face and rather ungainly, dangling arms.

"No one has ever offered me a cuppa before," he said with a puzzled look, then coiled like a corkscrew and vanished through the walls.

The following night Edna fell into a deep sleep. She was back in her childhood, laughing with her sister. The tensions of the past few weeks began to melt away when she heard the radio blast away again.

"Now, you know I don't care for that kind of noise, so switch it off," she called into the dark. "You may not need sleep, but I've had a rough time and now I'd like some peace. If you don't stop, we'll have words about it in the morning and don't expect to be resting then. Is that clear, eh?"

The radio tuned into reggae at top volume.

"God, you're a bully." Edna pulled the bedclothes tightly over her head and snuggled back in.

"You can try ignoring me, but it won't be for long! I'll have you off just like the rest! This is my house."

Edna sat up. "Wilfred, if you don't stop this nonsense, I will command you to go."

"Try it."

"I will!"

"No, don't," he replied quietly and the radio went off.

The next morning, while Edna was cleaning the kitchen, she whiffed him again. "Quite frankly, Wilfred, you pong. I was brought up on a farm and I'm used to disagreeable smells, but this is quite irregular. Have you never heard of a bath? Because if you're going to live here, you'd better scrub up.

"Don't start telling me what to do in my own house."

Edna raised her voice. "I think it's time we got this argument settled for good. This is not your house, Wilfred. This is my house. I bought it. Now get on with it. I don't care for the smell around here."

"And I don't care for your moralising. I've managed quite well scaring people off until you came here." He materialised next to her. "Why aren't you afraid of me?"

Edna sat down. "What are you going to do to me? You're nothing but a ghost; neither living nor properly dead."

"You're the only person who's ever spoken to me. The rest have run."

"Well, it's got lonely since my sister died."

"What was she like?" he asked, sitting down opposite her.

"Oh, we couldn't have been more different. Called

me skinny and stingy. When I think about all those cream cakes...I tried to reason with her, but she'd have none of it. In the end, her heart couldn't take it."

Edna snuffled, "I should have died before her, what with me being so much older." She closed her eyes, reminiscing. "Never thought I would miss her chatter so much. Always talked, our Maud did, never stopped. I used to say, 'For goodness sake give me break!' but now there's nothing but silence." She shuddered in the damp air, then opened her eyes and smiled mischievously.

"I remember, when we were kids, Maud was about five and I told her that everyone was allowed only so many words in a lifetime. She looked at me seriously, then closed her mouth; never said a word the whole week, not a word. Mother got frantic, until I confessed. Should have had a hiding, but dad laughed so much I got away with it."

Edna looked Wilfred in the eye. "Look, I don't mind you sticking around, but don't mess with me. I'll take no nonsense from an old scruff like you."

"How old are you, then?"

"If you had any manners, you'd know never to ask a lady her age."

"You're no lady," he sneered.

"No, you're right. I've had to work for my living. Anyway, if you must know, I'll be eighty-two next birthday."

"There you are! I am only seventy-five. A spring chicken."

"And the rest," Edna retorted.

"What do you mean?

"What I said. You may have snuffed it at seventy-five, but how long have you been stuck here? And, why are you here anyway?"

"None of your business."

"Have it your way. See if I care."

It had been a week since Edna had last seen, heard or sniffed her lodger. The house was quiet, only a roaring fire was crackling in the grate. She was sitting down repairing the hem of her skirt when she pricked her finger. She looked up.

"You're back, then?"

"Don't tell me you missed me."

"Missed your nuisance, but now you're here - make yourself useful. If you can knock over a cup of tea, you can make one."

"I'm not turning into your servant."

"I am not asking you to be my servant." She looked up and smiled. "You could be my friend, though."

"I wasn't friendly to people when I was alive. Why should I start now?"

"Ah, so that's your problem?"

Wilfred went quiet.

"I'm listening."

"I'm not talking."

"Oh, cut it out. A problem shared is a problem halved. I've told you mine, what's yours?"

"All right, if you must know, I can't go over because when I was alive I was a miserable, unfriendly, mean, spiteful chap."

"Oh, so nothing's changed?"

"Don't interrupt," he said, waving his arms about. "When my body died, I left, as one does, and went up this black tunnel; then got stuck. It was easier to come back here. At least I knew the house."

"Didn't anyone try to help you?"

"That's the point. No one would."

"I see," Edna nodded with understanding. "You never helped anyone when you were down here, so why should anyone help you when you got stuck up there. Hmm, interesting. Well, you know what you can do now, Willie, don't you?" Edna pointed to the kitchen. "You can start by putting the kettle on."

"Don't call me Willie."

Edna ignored him. "You have to start sometime or you'll stay here forever. Not a very nice prospect with all the changes taking place."

"What changes?" Wilfred looked startled.

"Well, they're talking about putting a new road through. That would mean knocking down the house. Won't bother me, I'll probably be gone by then and if not, well, they'll have to find me another place. Who's going to re-house a ghost?" She looked at Wilfred. His eyes were downcast and he was tugging at his beard nervously. "You're better off being my friend. If you behave yourself, I'll help you over." She smiled. "I like the odd prank myself. When we get up there, we'll have a ball! Mind you, I'm in no hurry."

Wilfred raised his head and slowly walked towards the kitchen.

"Tell me, Willie, does your hair continue to grow when you're a ghost? It's awfully long."

"Suppose so, never paid much attention to it."

"I can see that. Come over here. We'll do something about it."

Months passed and there was no sign of Edna moving out of Gorse Cottage. The lawns were neatly cut, the collapsed fence repaired, hedges trimmed and along the border, a row of red roses flourished under expert care.

There were no visitors. The postman left the odd bill in the box by the gate and the milkman didn't call. Edna continued her daily walks into the village, buying what she needed at Bob Smith's store. Once a week she called for her pension at the post office. The moment she walked in, the locals would stop talking, whisper or noticeably change the subject and stare. It was obvious that something was going on, but they were too cowardly to ask. Edna did nothing to help.

Eventually, curiosity got the better of them and Edna suspected that the storekeeper was put in charge. His manner towards her changed and he became the epitome of solicitousness and gallantry. She gathered that if he found out, he would become a local hero and his custom would increase.

One late afternoon she ran out of sugar. "How silly of me to forget," she told Wilfred. She often talked to him, whether he was there or not and invariably, he would turn up. She dressed carefully, putting her best coat on, then wrapped a shawl around her shoulders and walked to the store. By the time she arrived, it was closing time and Bob Smith was tidying up.

"Just some sugar, please," Edna said. "My memory

doesn't seem so good these days."

"That's all right, Mrs. Bright, many a folk would be proud to be as nimble as you are. Now, let me help you." He placed the sugar into a carrier and, locking up the shop, lead her out. "I have some business your way, Mrs. Bright, let me carry your bag for you."

Edna teased him a smile. The timing was perfect; she would lead him on a little, then play her trump card.

"So, how is business these days, Mr. Smith?" she asked before he had a chance to address her.

"Thank you for asking, Mrs. Bright. Could be better, but mustn't complain. And how..?"

She silenced him with her next question. "Of course, times are hard. Don't you find that is the case with all small businesses?"

Bob Smith swallowed hard. It was clear he did not like the reference to a small business, but he had his own game to play. He tried again. "And how...?"

"Of course, most people have cars and stock up in supermarkets," Edna continued, suppressing a chuckle.

After a while they both fell into silence, Edna marching in a sprightly step with the shopkeeper in tow. By the time they reached the riverbank, the sun had dipped behind the hills and twilight had set in. Edna slowed down and waited for Bob Smith to catch his breath.

"You don't mind taking a shortcut through the woods, Mr. Smith, do you?"

Bob Smith opened his mouth then shut it again.

"You see, the path through the woods is considerably shorter and cuts out the main road," Edna said walking on, knowing that the man behind her was gritting his teeth.

When they reached her cottage, she stopped by a new gate. Alongside it, a lilac tree weighed heavily with the scent of its blossoms. "Well, thank you for carrying the bag for me," Edna said, opening the gate. "I wonder, would you like to come in for a cup of tea?"

Bob Smith's furrows creased with delight. "That's awfully nice of you, Mrs. Bright. I'd love one. And how are you enjoying living at Gorse Cottage?" he blurted out at last.

"Oh, fine, thank you for asking this long time. You see, Wilfred is a most helpful chap. I don't know how I would have managed without him."

Redemption

Niti Jain

I am twenty-two years old. As I look at myself in the mirror now, in this dark cold room, I realise I look much older. Much older than the people I grew up with. I would have said I look much older than my friends, but I can't - I never had any. I was like this invisible boy walking around in the school. No one spoke to me, and when someone did, I didn't know what to say. I always felt like I would say something wrong. I kept quiet.

I remember being quiet for a very long time. It was that one day when I shouldn't have. That one day when I should have spoken up. Had I spoken up that day, I wouldn't be standing here looking at my image reflecting its old self.

I was twelve years old and it was Christmas. Like every year we were at Grandma Rose's house in the small village she chose to stay in. I, my brother James, and cousin Maggie always had a great time there, till

James started behaving weird and grownup. I loved being at Grandma Rose's house. It was a huge house and we all got a room to ourselves.

She had a huge garden with a lot of colourful flowers. There was a stream that ran down right at the back of the house. I often sat there with Maggie and talked about the sky, the birds and school and the guy she liked and the girl I liked. She was a year younger than me, but she was very smart. She knew geography and history and she wrote poems. I remember she sang one of her poems that Christmas.

She killed herself.

In the last ten years I've thought about her a lot. I often thought about how it feels to kill yourself. What must have gone through her mind? What must she have been thinking when she decided that dying was better than being alive? I never came to a conclusion. I often tried doing it myself. A lot of times I sat with a razor in my hand to slit that vein on my wrist – but I couldn't. I couldn't do it. It was difficult. I was scared. I could never decide if living a long life hating yourself was more difficult than that one moment of ending it.

Is it brave to kill yourself or is it cowardice? Is it brave because you refuse to live a life on any other terms than your own or is it cowardice because you did not stand up for yourself and fight back? Is it brave because you would rather die than live a life of guilt or is it cowardice because you didn't speak up when you could and there seems to be no other way? I could never find an answer.

I think it takes that one moment of self-loathing and self-pity that makes you do it. That one moment that overshadows all reasoning about the right and the wrong - when you find the courage to slit that vein. I never found it.

She did. She killed herself because of me.

It was the day after Christmas. Grandma Rose's friend, Mrs. Jenkins, always hosted a lunch the day after Christmas. She invited all the grown up people from our house too. We liked the home to ourselves. We felt like grownups being in the huge house on our own.

Maggie and I made some sandwiches and decided to sit by the stream and eat them. James was on the phone with his girlfriend. I was scared of him. He was six years older than me. He wasn't always this weird but of late Maggie and I usually tried to avoid him. We waited for him to hang up and asked him if he wanted to come.

"James? Do you want to come out with us by the stream for lunch? We made sandwiches," I said.

"I am not interested in you and your stupid conversations," he said, rolling his eyes and dialling another number.

We shrugged our shoulders.

"Let's go," I said to Maggie.

"Why don't you go and I'll take a quick shower and come out in ten minutes."

"OK," I said, picking up the sandwiches.

I went to sit by the stream waiting for Maggie to come out. It was a beautiful sky. The trees and the stream were covered with white snow. There was sun. I didn't realise how much time had passed. I looked at my watch and it had been half an hour that I was sitting there alone and I was starving.

I got up, picked up the sandwiches and walked back in to the house. I put the sandwiches back in the kitchen and went up the stairs to look for Maggie. I could hear her. I couldn't make out what she was saying. The door was ajar. I saw her lying on the bed, clutching the bedcover, naked, trying to shout. No words escaped from the cloth stuffed in her mouth - just a faint cry. I saw James, on top of her, naked.

She saw me standing there and she tried to lift her arm but James held it tight in place. Her face was red and wet. I looked into her eyes for a moment. She closed them. I still dream of her eyes sometimes - wide, brown eyes, pleading, sad, horrified and painful. I stood there. Quiet. I should have said something. I saw James stagger up and walk towards me buttoning up his jeans. He threw a towel on my face and said, "One word kid and you know what I'll do. So just stay quiet."

Stay quiet. And I did. When our parents came back, Maggie refused to come down. She stayed in her room saying she wasn't too well. I kept quiet. Two days later, she slit her vein with a blade from James' razor. I still kept quiet.

I have been quiet since. It has been suffocating. If only I could have found the courage to say it out loud I would have been free. Maggie might still be here. Can you imagine living in a locked closet for ten years? Every moment feels like a decade, living as the guy who could have saved someone but didn't, because he was scared. It was that one moment when I could have spoken up or the last ten years that I spent regretting it.

It was that same moment when Maggie used that blade, and I still regret it.

I went through that self-loathing everyday for ten years. That makes people want to kill themselves and yet I still did not find the courage to use that blade. It's not easy to live with guilt - guilt for someone's death. Can you imagine what she must have gone through to have done it? I found the courage today - to use that blade.

I killed James. I cut a vein right through his neck.

And now, as I stand in this cold dark room, with James on the couch in the pool of blood, looking at my reflection in the mirror, I smile. I laugh. My reflection looks free. It feels like I am out of that closet. I know I have killed for justice - for Maggie. May her soul rest in peace and may my soul be redeemed.

Miss Margaret Jones

Clare Scott

I used to live in that house. But I kept it very differently. I grew old in that house and we were a very respectable family with a well-respected business in the town. It was in my father's family for several generations and we lived there very comfortably. I was the last of the line to live there, holding on to the last. I am proud of the way I managed to hang on, being the keeper of the family 'mansion'. But it's not quite a mansion.

It was built in the nineteenth century for my father's grandfather, a butcher. It was in the time when our town was prosperous and businesses were growing, when people had money to spend and wanted to show it off. That's why the house has such a grand door and windows taller and wider than a man. It's the biggest house in the street. It was a house built for large family parties, for celebrations, for meetings, for births and for deaths. We had a smart parlour, a dining room and a sitting room, with a piano and our furniture was large to fill the space. We even had a Jacobean sideboard and cabinet in one of the front rooms, dark heavy oak they were, with candy-twist legs.

My favourite spot was in a small armchair just to the side of the middle window upstairs, where I would sit in the first morning sunlight and look down onto the road, watching the townsfolk passing by, stopping and chatting part way through their shopping and stumbling home from the Rose and Crown after ten in the evenings. Our house was taller than the opposite row, so I could watch without being overseen. That felt good too. Although we were sociable, we kept our position, having shutters to close across the windows, with thick nets draped behind these and then heavy velvet curtains. That kept a sense of decent privacy.

The family that lives here now is nothing like we used to be. They have different ways that seem very foreign to me. I don't like change when it disrupts the peace and stability of a place. I especially don't like it when their machinery shakes the walls and with such a racket of hammering and sawing that you can't hear yourself think. I don't see why you have to alter a place to such a degree that it loses all the dignity and stature it grew into over the years. Where's the respect? It makes me very agitated and I feel so helpless, because I can't tell them to stop. They won't listen because I'm not the owner. I'm just that old woman who lived here until she was 103.

You could tell that we were a family to tip your hat to. They all stopped to pay their regards when they saw us. The local chapel sent visitors at least once a week. I enjoyed their visits, hearing the gossip and how the choir was singing. Even when I had my hundredth birthday, they were still calling and bringing me tasty cakes, to bring a song to my heart – as they used to say. I hated it when my strength petered out and those last three years of my life, when my world as I had always known it faded away from me.

The new family, though, they are different folk from away, they have different ways. They don't seem to care that anyone can see in and the windows are bare, exposing their lives to the rest of the world. They leave the lights on all hours, day and night and they are so loud. The colours they have painted the walls, we were always so restrained and sophisticated in our tastes. And heating – in my day we only needed the one storage heater in the hall for the whole house – but they've put in radiators everywhere.

I feel as if they have made my family invisible, removing the evidence that we ever existed. I get so het up sometimes, I want to shout at them and tell them what I think of them, but they won't hear me. They're so busy with their hectic lives that I and mine have been ironed out, wiped clean as if we had never existed. I wish I could make them listen to me and show some respect for all that we worked so hard to create. Sometimes I wish I could stand straight in front of them and tell them what for. How do I stop them from making changes that permanently alter a once beautiful home?

I don't care for the way the oldest girl dresses, either.

She doesn't seem to have any self respect, with clothes that look as if she never washes them and cut to show off bits that would be better covered up. I can't stand their music either, we would never have had it like that, so that the walls seem to shake with the noise. She has such a beautiful singing voice that she only uses when she's alone in her bedroom. I wish she would use it. I blame the parents myself. The way they let them do as they please. I don't see any sign of respect from the children, no "please" or "thank you".

Sometimes I do try to make myself known to them. I have tried. I enter their sitting room and come close up, but they don't see me or hear me. The mother often complains that the room has got a cold draught and turns up the heating, but that is the only effect that I have. I pass through their walls, viewing all that they are doing, but they can't even sense my disapproval. It's so frustrating not being heard and not being able to put a stop to it all. Last night I did feel some small success though. I was so distressed by the horror film they were watching on the television, I felt I had to do something, so I used all my will to turn out the lights. There was a flicker and a slight click and everything went dark. And they screamed. It was very satisfying. Next I'm going to have a go at the boiler, I think.

Toothy Moose Bar

Megan Power

In my bedside table drawer there's an
Undated but must be around 1998 letter from
Another existence in which you call me
My Everything

I haven't been anyone's everything
Since

Alright that's not quite accurate
I have
But it was mostly situational
Highly geographical and ultimately fictional

Duodecuple winters snow past
We meet again finally
Blast of dubstep, scotch, electric heat
The new basement bar on old Argyle
A street we stumbled arm in arm down many
Nights in another existence

Sitting now adultly round a
Reproduction pub table in the trendy Toothy Moose
After ginger hugs, the group deliciously bitching about

Parking garage price gouging and an impending blizzard,
You and I trade looks, the bar begins to swelter
Sticking a cigarette in my mouth like
A pacifier I stride outside
Before coming to a boil

Argyle Street is a gleaming layer of black ice
Sprinkled with tiny rocks of salt
Fat wet flurries twist on the harbour wind

Logical to assume love dies
But ours?
Spent all those winters just hibernating
Docile and suspended in time
Patiently awaiting its late arriving spring

Or maybe in like a coma
Roiling blackness and the threat of death
Suddenly supplanted by a groggy daybreak awakening
To the surprised joy of attendants

Midway down page two
The heart ripper goes
All I ever wanted to do was make you happy
and I thank you for that chance

It doesn't ring cliché
Since I was Your Everything
And we're talking 1998

The world was wide and wild to me then
And I jetted out into it
Zigzagging around until the proof mounted:
How very small and tame things actually are
Everywhere worth being is pretty much the same

Are you the same?
You must be
People don't change, you know
They only become more themselves

All the places I want to travel to these days are
Invisible and interior

In closing
You signed the letter *2 Pac*
Who hung shirtless and insouciant on my that era wall
And finally you drew a sad face with coloured in tears

All those winters stormed by
Yet like a front lawn, like fish under ice,
Our apparently dead love's still alive

Burn

Anthony Jones

The melting conflagration
Led to my disintegration,
A trial of devastation
From a miniscule combustion.

I awoke, and was a
Blistered slab
Of meat
Upon the butcher's table
And screaming for my mother.

Maxed out on morphine
It did not assuage the pain.
I saw my burnt-out, scorching thigh
Pulsating through the cellophane

I stood before the mirror then
To find I'd been erased.
My fingerprints were not my own
And neither was my face.

My Shadow

Sarada Thompson

Even in my early memories I remember
Playing with my shadow,
Walking, running, skipping and dancing.
Fascinated as it shimmered short and long-tall
And as it sometimes almost disappeared,
In dawn, midday, dusk and nightfall,
Walking, running, skipping and dancing.
My friend, my shadow and me.
In youth, my shadow wore stiletto heels
And took a different shape,
Striding, running, skipping and dancing.
As an adult with family, my shadow mimicking me
Carrying a baby and holding on to a toddler,
Walking, running, skipping and dancing.
Now my shadow is walking, running, skipping and
dancing,
But where am I?
My shadow grows stronger but I will pounce on it and
I will be
Walking, running, skipping and dancing,
For you are just
M.S.
My Shadow!

Dial

Martina Davies

Gorweddodd y bachgen bochgoch ar ei wely â'i galon yn dychlamu'n wyllt yn erbyn ei frest. Roedd ei wallt fflamgoch yn nyth o gwrls ar ei ben a'r smotiau coch ar ei wyneb fel llosgfynyddoedd yn briwio o dan y croen. Gorweddodd a'i ddwylo wedi'i twcio'n dynn o dan ei ben ôl mewn ymdrech i anghofio am yr hyn y bu'n gwneud y noson cynt. Y dwylo oedd ar fai!

Bachgen swil, deunaw oed oedd Huw, roedd yn dueddol o gadw ei hun i'w hun. Yr un oedd y stori yn yr ysgol, nid oedd ganddo ryw lawer o ffrindiau a phan fyddai rhai o'r merched yn gwneud sbort am ei ben, eistedd yn unig mewn cornel a'i drwyn pigog wedi'i gladdu yn nyfnder rhyw lyfr gwyddonol y gwnâi Huw. Efallai nad Huw oedd y bachgen mwyaf golygus yn yr ysgol, ond yn sicr, ef oedd y bachgen clyfra!

Wrth i'r noson dynnu amdani, gorweddodd Huw yn anesmwyth ar ei wely a'i feddwl ym mhell, bell o'r

Revenge

Martina Davies

The boy lay on his bed, his heart trembling in his chest. His red hair a nest of curls and the spots on his face like miniature volcanoes brewing under his skin. He lay with his hands tucked tight under his back in an effort to forget about what they had been doing the night before. The hands were to blame!

Huw was a shy boy, only eighteen, and he tended to keep to himself. The story was the same in school. He didn't have many friends, and when some of the girls would laugh at him, Huw would sit quietly in the corner taking it all in. His spiky nose stuck into a clumpy book about physics. Maybe Huw wasn't the most popular of people, but he sure was the cleverest.

As the night closed in about him, Huw lay uncomfortably, his mind a long way away as he relived the vicious events of last night.

ddaear wrth iddo ail-fyw digwyddiadau erchyll y noson gynt.

Roedd ei lygaid yn ddu ac yn llawn ofn fel dwy ogof dywyll yn arwain at ddyfnderoedd ei feddyliau.

Daliodd y dwylo gwelw'n agos i'w lygaid gan edrych ar yr holl grychau man a oedd yn dal ei ddyfodol, yn creu ystyr i'w fodolaeth. Y crychau oedd hefyd yn dal y gyfrinach. Llifodd y meddyliau yn ôl i'w ben fel ton yn llenwi'r harbwr gan ddanfon ias oer dros ei gorff fel pla wrth iddo gofio am y noson honno...

Nos Sadwrn oedd hi. Roedd y dre'n orlawn, y lleuad yn llawn a phawb yn barod i fwynhau mewn rhyw dafarn neu glwb...oni bai am Huw.

Y noson honno roedd gan Huw drefniadau amgenach. Casglodd yr offer at ei gilydd yn ofalus a'i rhoi yn y cwdyn du mor dynner, fel mam yn rhoi ei phlentyn i gysgu. Tynnodd y menig yn dyn am ei ddwylo. Y menig a fyddai'n cario'r bai. Nid oedd Huw yn cymryd un risg heno. Roedd wedi bod yn paratoi yn gynnil am y noson hon ers misoedd...ers y noson y cyfarfododd â hi...cofiodd am y llygaid glas a fu mor las y bu bron iddo syrthio i'w canol, y gwefusau melys, melfedaidd a'r dwylo esmwyth a wnaeth i'w galon gyflymu gyda phob cyffyrddiad. Ond yng nghefn ei feddwl roedd yr un hen eiriau swrth a'r un hen atebion sych y bu'n troelli yn ei gof ers blynyddoedd. Roedd ei galon yn llawn dicter. Tynnodd y got ddu amdano a chau'r drws yn glep ar ei ôl.

Arhosodd yn yr union fan ar hyd y llwybr lle yr ooedd wedi aros troeon o'r blaen. Ond gwahanol oedd ei fwriad heno. Arhosodd yn dawel tu ôl i gysgod y

His eyes were black and fearful like two caves leading to the pit of his thoughts.

He held his white hands close to his eyes looking at all the creases which hold his past and future. The creases which also hold the secret. His thoughts filled his head like a wave of water filling a harbour sending a cold chill down his body as he remembered the night before.

It was a Saturday night, the town was overflowing, the moon full and everyone was ready to have a good night...everyone but Huw.

That night, Huw had other plans. He collected the equipment together and put them into the black bag so delicately, like a mother putting her child to bed. He pulled the black gloves on tight. The gloves that would carry the blame for what he was about to do. Huw was taking no risk tonight. He had been planning this for a long time, since he had met her. He remembered her blue eyes which were so blue he had nearly drowned in them, the sweet lips and the velvet hands which made his heart race with every touch. But in the back of his mind were the same old harsh words, the same old answers which had been stirring in his head for so long. His heart was full of loathing. He pulled the black coat tight about him and closed the door with a thud.

He waited at the same lane he had waited times before. But his plan was different tonight. He hid in the shade of the big oak tree, his breath heavier tonight than any other night. It was pitch black and only the lights from the town were to be seen. Huw watched the leaves crumble with the wind, the trees overhead

dderwen fawr a honno'n wyrdd gan fywyd. Roedd ei
anadl yn drymach heno na'r un noson arall. Roedd hi'n
ddu bost erbyn hyn a dim ond golau'r dre yn rhes yn y
pellter fel trên y nos yn goleuo'r llwybr bach cul.
Gwyliodd Huw'r dail ar hyd y llwybr yn crebachu
gyda'r awel a'r coed uwch ei ben fel bwystfilod yn
hisian yn fygythiol yn y gwynt, fel petaent yn gwybod
beth oedd bwriad Huw.

Edrychodd ar ei oriawr, 2.20 yb. *Dim hir nawr,*
meddyliodd wrth iddo ddechrau teimlo'n ansicr.
Roedd ei wyneb yn welw yn erbyn y nos a'r awyr mor
ddu â'r fagddu. Gwelwodd ei wyneb fel pluen wen
mewn pwll o darmac gwlyb am eiliad wrth iddo
feddwl am yr hyn oedd ar fin gwneud. Yna, heb un
rhybudd, atseiniodd sŵn y sodlau'n finiog trwy'r
tywyllwch gan ddihuno'r nos o'i drwm gwsg. Cododd
Huw ei draed yn drwsgl a chamu'n ôl i mewn i
ddirgelwch y cysgodion.

Tyfodd cysgod siapus y wraig ar hyd y llwybr.
Dyma oedd Huw wedi bod yn aros amdano. Yr holl
baratoi. Y gwylio a'r disgwyl. Yr holl weithiau y bu'n
gofyn am ddawns, neu ofyn am ddêt, ond bob tro yn
clywed yr un atebion dideimlad a'r un hen esgusodion
anniolchgar. Roedd wedi hen alaru ar fod yn
unig...dyma oedd ei gyfle ef i ddial a'i tro hwy i dalu'r
pris.

Cydiodd Huw yn dynn yn y bibell gadarn yn ei law
a'i ddal gyda'i holl nerth yn barod i drywanu.

hissing threateningly, like they knew what Huw was about to do.

He looked at his watch: 2:20 a.m. *Not long now*, Huw thought to himself as he started feeling unsure. His face was white against the night and the sky as black as coal. His face whitened even more for a moment as he thought of what he was about to do. Then, without a warning, her heels echoed in the distance, wakening the night from its sleep. Huw stepped back into the shadows, ready.

Her shapely shadow grew nearer and nearer along the lane. This is what Huw had been waiting for. All his preparation would finally pay off. All the times he had asked for a dance, a kiss, a date, but all the while had heard the same ungrateful excuses. He was tired of being lonely...this was his chance for revenge and their time to pay the price.

Huw tightened his grasp on the pipe in his hand and held it with all his might, ready to strike.

Free Fall

Annie Bell-Davies

When I found the letter in the back pocket of his jeans, my mind shut itself off from the washing. The host of other chores that had piled up during the week were forgotten. They piled up every week, waiting for my weekends; my free days. Free! That's a laugh. Free, perhaps, to do the shopping; queuing and jostling in the local supermarket for the ingredients for a happy home and a contented family. Then to spend the rest of my free time running around in circles tidying and cleaning, catering and ironing; to sit exhausted on a Sunday night dreading the next day when the monotony would start again. The job that had saved me from insanity within these walls had become my worst nightmare. The little luxuries my salary brought had somehow reinvented themselves as necessities, and I was as trapped in a boring and demoralising job as I had been at home. I was spiralling downwards and I was near the bottom, I was sure.

And there I was getting another load ready for the wash. Jeans. It's always jeans. I don't know where they all come from. It was Saturday. The shopping was done, the cupboards full again ready for the onslaught that would come when the football match, the shopping trip and the sleepover came to an end and my family made their leisurely way home. It was raining. I was alone.

Men never clear out their pockets when they dump their laundry in the linen bin, or on the floor, or most annoyingly, on the floor next to the linen bin. I learned that lesson soon after I was married seventeen years ago. I managed to put two ten pound notes through the spinner and had to iron them back into a presentable state, because in those days, to present them was a must. I have always checked John's pockets since then - just in case.

That's when I found it, folded and tucked out of sight in his back pocket. I knew what it was just by the feel of the expensive envelope. It was as though the quality of the paper held its own sense of morality that sent out a silent alarm, like a government health warning on the side of a pack of cigarettes. *Reading this can seriously affect your marriage,* it seemed to say. The envelope had his name written on it in brown ink. Inside, the paper was the same pale peach colour as the envelope and the edges of the single sheet were scalloped. A wave of envy washed over me at the extravagance that allowed her to be stylish. How dare she be stylish! I had no time to be stylish. I had no time to write. I had no time.

Perhaps I should have hesitated before reading it.

John and I had always respected each other's privacy but that was because there had been trust. Suddenly there wasn't any trust. In the middle of the kitchen floor, on a pile of dirty jeans, I sat and allowed my eyes to devour her words.

I read it quickly and calmly. Then, I read it again. On the second reading, I got angry and by the time I read it for the third time, absorbing every syllable of her love, I was physically sick. My lovely track suit was sodden so I tore it off and pushed everything hurriedly into the washing machine along with the jeans and pressed the buttons. The gentle hum of the machine blocked, for a moment, her voice in my head.

The kettle boiled quickly and I made myself some coffee, hot and sweet the way I liked it; sugar instead of sweeteners. There would be no more concessions to his little whims.

Naked and furious, I sat repeating her words over and over again in my mind.

When you leave her...we will be so happy...together... forever...love you...my little Sugar Monkey. Sugar Monkey! Never in my life have I thought of John as my little Sugar Monkey. Perhaps I should have. No, it's too ridiculous. I could almost laugh; almost.

It's funny because I didn't cry. No, I didn't cry until much later when Chloe came home. Angry as I was at finding the letter, I could not feign shock and somewhere in the mix of emotions that churned in my stomach, there was relief. I knew then that I hadn't been imagining things. I had blamed myself for being suspicious of the overtime, the hurried, cryptic phone calls, the texts and all those clean shirts and new ties. I had chastised myself for not trusting him. So, it was a relief to know that I was not mad. I had been right and for all the best reasons I had blamed myself and believed in him. The bastard!

"Mum!"

Poor Chloe. The sight of her mother sitting naked in the kitchen must have frightened her.

"Mum, are you alright?" she asked, moving ever so tentatively towards me, like she was afraid of this strange phenomenon before her.

"I was sick so I put my clothes in the washing machine," I told her calmly, as if trying to reassure her with the logic of my actions.

"Are you ok? Do you still feel sick? Do you want me to call the doctor?" She didn't give me a chance to answer because she had reached me and touched my arm.

"You're freezing!" she exclaimed. "How long ago were you sick?"

I tried to laugh, to give the impression that it was nothing, but my words came out more like a cough: "Half past one."

"But it's quarter to four. You need to get warm. Can you walk upstairs or do you want me to fetch something to put on? Shall I phone Dad?"

"No." I said it with more emphasis than I had meant and Chloe eyed me with suspicion.

She was concerned. My little girl was so concerned that finally I cried. Like a baby I sobbed and screamed and in the warmth of her arms I felt comforted and loved - at last I felt loved. Soon it would be me comforting her but for now I borrowed some of her strength.

Calmer, I went upstairs and put on an old jumper and skirt, the first things that came to hand, and I was just running a comb through my greying auburn hair when I saw Chloe standing in the doorway.

"What's wrong Mum?"

How could I say nothing? My husband, her father, was having an affair. Not just a passing fling but a full-blown love affair where the idea of leaving us had been discussed - planned even. I shivered at the thought of them together, discussing and deciding my fate and the children's as though we had no say in the matter. But Chloe was too young to hear my thoughts; too young to understand what grown-ups do to each other in their own beds and others. She loved her Daddy. How could I distort and destroy that love? Twelve is too young to hear such truths.

"Nothing," I said at last; putting off the moment until I was stronger. "I just felt ill for a bit. I'm alright now," I smiled a shallow smile and asked her to go and put the kettle on. When she had gone, I sat in front of the mirror and stayed there until John came in.

He was late coming home. Probably stopped with her for a quickie, I thought bitterly. But I was glad he was late. It had given me time to recoup my strength and armed with the truth, I felt powerful enough to face him.

"Why isn't tea ready?" he demanded. No hello, no how are you? No kiss. There were never any kisses.

"Because I haven't made it yet," I told him and I began to comb my hair again. It gave me something to do with my hands, stopped me from slapping the hard-done-by expression off his indignant face.

"Well hurry up, love, I'm starving." His tone had changed. He had sensed my mood, recognised trouble and done a U-turn, typical John.

"I thought perhaps we could all go out for a meal tonight." I made the suggestion quite sweetly, I thought.

"Don't be silly. You know we can't afford it," he coaxed, on edge now his wallet was threatened. I always knew how to hurt John.

"Well if you stopped buying all those new ties, John, you might be able to treat us sometimes too."

The ties had been presents from her. I knew it, we both did, and in that instant he knew that I had found out. I could see him question himself. How? When? What had he said or done to give the game away? What was he to do?

I watched him squirm. He had never been spontaneous; he couldn't think on his feet and I enjoyed his discomfort with an unfair and unexpected pleasure.

Then, when he spoke at last, I was almost proud of him.

"You know," he said simply. At least he wasn't going to put me through the indignity of more lies.
"How?" he asked.

"That's not important," I told him, not prepared to tell him where he'd gone wrong. Arming a man with that sort of information would be like tying the knot in the noose that is going to hang you! I watched as he sank onto the bed as though his strength had been sapped and his legs could no longer bear his weight. I felt cold inside, but above all I felt as though I had gained control. And I liked it. My life was in my hands again and I had to decide what I wanted to do with it before my control and my nerve were engulfed again by my apathy. I saw it quite clearly. I had two choices: I could stay or I could go. Forgive, or not forgive.

But who was I kidding? As I sat there looking at the man I had married all those years before, I realised that the choice had already been made. It had been made by him. Our marriage did not fulfil him; he had gone elsewhere and in my heart I could not bring myself to blame him. Sometimes the only way to go is out. We had lived with each other for years but we had not been together for a long time.

He looked up at me then and our eyes met. He had always had nice eyes, not stunningly blue or seductively dark, just kind, gentle eyes. Not the eyes of a man who would deliberately hurt, but there was no love in them for me, and without words we nodded and agreed; the wasting was over. The spiral had stopped.

If Only

Niti Jain

She sat in the rocking chair across from me. She kept looking out the window and I kept looking at her. If only she'd look at me and give me another chance.

"I'm sorry Sherry," I said.

She didn't answer.

"Look, I know it's my fault and I should not have gone to Vegas, but..."

The phone rang and she walked past me to take the call in the kitchen.

I didn't follow her. There was no point. I just looked at her. I loved her from the first day I saw her. I ruined it all.

Every time I close my eyes, I still see her as I did the first time.

***

I walked into the cafe to meet my friend, Adil. I was scanning the place for him when I saw her. She sat beside a window with sunlight falling on her face. She rolled a strand of hair around her finger and tucked it behind her ear. It let itself loose and fell on her face again. She held a book in her hand which she wasn't reading. She looked out the window, lost. She looked like a princess who came to this era by mistake and had no idea why she was here. She was beautiful. Just when I was contemplating going up to her, my phone beeped. It was Adil.

"Dan? Dude, I crashed my car."

"What? Are you alright?"

"Yeah I'm fine. But the car's dead."

"Where are you?" I asked as I looked at her once more and ran out of the cafe.

***

"Hello?" I heard her part of the conversation.

"Adil? How are you?"

"Yes. I am fine."

"No, Adil. I don't feel like going out."

"I know. But Dan..."

There was a long pause on this side of the conversation.

"I know. I just don't feel like..." she said again.

"You're right."

"I'll see you there."

"Seven is fine," she said, looking at her watch.

She came back in the living room and stood in front of the window holding her coffee mug.

"Are you going out?" I asked.

She turned around and walked out of the room, without answering.

It's not like she doesn't love me anymore. I know she still does. But things have changed. If only I had listened to her and not gone on that trip. Things would have probably been the same. If only I hadn't... It hurts to see her like that. I still live in this house we bought together, but she doesn't notice me anymore. It's like she wants to forget I even exist. If only I had not gone to Vegas.

**

I went to that cafe everyday at the same time, hoping to find her again. I found her there on the eighteenth day, at the same table, with the same posture and the same book. I walked up to her and stood there for a good minute before she looked at me.

She tilted her head to the left and raised an eyebrow. That was all she did to ask me who I was and what I was doing there.

"Umm...Do you mind if I...?" I asked, pointing towards the empty seat across from her.

She looked at the seat, she looked at me. She looked like a lost princess.

"No. Go ahead. I was just leaving anyway."

"Oh. No. I didn't mean to...I was just..."

She tilted her head and raised her eyebrow again.

What was I thinking? I thought.

"I was wondering if you knew where I could buy that book. I've been looking for that one for a long time."

She looked at the book in her hand

"Really? What is it about?"

"Umm...I...uh..." I tried to say something, anything, scratching my head.

She smiled. And that was the beginning.

***

I stood at the door watching her get dressed and putting on makeup. I knew she didn't want to go out. I knew she would.

Not long before, she would have been laughing and smiling at me while she got dressed. She would turn around and look at me at the doorway and ask, "Is this one fine?"

"Yes sweetheart. You look great."

"Are you sure?"

And she would change irrespective of what I said.

I stood there looking at her. She didn't look at me. She didn't ask me anything.

"You look great," I said.

She walked past me, picked up the car keys and left. I watched her leaving, without a word. It hurts so much to let go of the one you love. It hurts more when you know it's your fault. I wish I could hold her and tell her I was sorry. I wish I could hug her and tell her it was all going to be fine. I wish I could ask for another chance. I couldn't. It was my fault.

***

"Do you believe in God?" she asked me.
"No."
"Devil?"
"No."
"Hmmm..." she said thoughtfully.
"Parallel universe?"
"You mean ghosts and spirits?"
"Yes."
"No. But maybe there is another world out there in space."
"Why don't you believe in God?"
"I don't have a reason to."
"Hmmm..." she said again.
"Well, this book is about religion and parallel universes. I am not sure if you were looking for this one," she said.
She left me speechless again. But then she smiled. And that first awkward conversation was a beginning to the beautiful five years that followed.

***

I waited for her, sitting in her rocking chair, looking at the stars outside. Just being in that chair felt like being close to her. I wanted to talk to her. If only she would listen. I heard her turn the key in the door. She came in with Adil. He was my friend but I was jealous. I know he was just trying to be helpful but I should have been the one making things better for her. But wasn't I the one who got her in this position, in the first place.

They went straight to the kitchen. I kept sitting on the chair, very still, so that I could listen to them talking.

"For how long do you think you can keep ignoring everyone?"

"I don't know Adil. I know no one says anything. But I can see it in their eyes. They look at me in a weird way. Their eyes ask me questions. What am I to say?"

"Just ignore them. It wasn't your fault."

"I know it wasn't my fault. I don't know what to do. I kept telling him not to go to Vegas. We would be getting married in a week if he..." she started crying.

***

I got up from the rocking chair to go out on the balcony. I could not see her in so much pain because of me. I wanted to hold her, kiss her and tell her I loved her. But I ruined it. I ruined my life and her future.

***

Adil came out to the living room. She followed him with the two coffee mugs.

"What's the matter?" she asked. "What are you staring at...?"

They both looked at the rocking chair.

"Th-that chair. Why is it moving? Is someone else home?" Adil asked.

She shook her head.

***

If only I hadn't gone to Vegas. If only I hadn't had so much to drink. If only I didn't drive.

I wish I could tell her about the parallel universe. And that it did exist.

Unknown Door

Sarada Thompson

In the midst of a dark spiralling abyss of void, I saw eerie shadows all lurking in a myriad of shapes, elongating and swirling about. There I was, not knowing how I had got there and as I was trying to comprehend, found these forms in the dimness closing in with a menace. Fear of the unknown slowly took its grip, as I realised I could not feel my body. I was just feelings and emotions and thoughts, but where was my body? Panic! This shock could kill me! Slowly as the imminent figures prowled even closer, I realised it was futile to cry out, as I did not have a voice: not that that would have helped!

Somewhere in that chasm, in the mind and feelings which existed, stirred a distant memory of a reliable tool - a word. The esoteric resonance of repeating the seed of the word grew into a tower and threw off the shadows and a spark glinted in the total darkness. Determined and growing into and glued into the incessant chants, in a non-existent body, beautiful stars twinkled all around at first in silver, then in a kaleidoscope of rainbow colour and merged into a sparkling fountain of bright iridescence.

It was a joy! If it was hell or purgatory just before, this must be a heaven of some kind. The awareness brought home a consciousness that this was just the other side of the coin: the existence which was me was enjoying this so much that I could have stayed here forever.

Just then something swung and in the midst, from the shimmering glistening to the gulf of gloom, right smack in the middle was, I became aware of, me! Conscious of being caught in a pendulum of opposites in this space of polarities, 'I' clung on to the key, sound of the hum of the word which I could see may help me from where there had once been a door for me to have slipped through. As that cognisant dawned on me, I could feel a throb of a heartbeat which seemed to come from within and yet seemed all about.

I must have had a nightmare, for I awoke with my heartbeat resounding in my ears, but my eyes were glued shut as slowly I could feel my body. I lay in bed for a long time, appreciating feeling my legs, arms, chest and stomach, my neck and head – and, in time, my whole body. I must have had a nightmare. Or maybe it was a glimpse.

Midwinter

Clare Scott

This is the time of death in frozen lands.
The earliest hours of day in blanket night,
When hope departed, no delays, the sands
Of time have run right through, all lies have taken flight,
The point of no return, when movement stilled
In lightless, lifeless, soundless, craggy cave,
The close to life's distractions, dreams fulfilled,
When merciless end comes to all you crave,
The last threshold is crossed, now face your shames.
Ice seizes the earth with bright crystals of quartz,
Trees stripped, bone bare skeletal frames,
The princess sleeps, locked in her tower, no thoughts.
This is no more than a soul's move to wane,
A breath released, before life starts again.

Little Hands

Rachel Coles

"Come here," he gestured, his voice deep but soft. "You've got little hands, haven't you?"

I strained to look at my hands in the dim light of the stables. They seemed an acceptable size to me. They were not little. They were not large. Just fourteen-year-old hands as my fourteen-year-old eyes saw them. I closed the stable yard gate and made my way to where Mick was leaning against the white pickup truck. It was getting dark and cold.

"I've got a job for you, Kel."

He sucked the last ember from the pathetically thin roly and stared at it with disappointment as if by some miracle it would reignite.

"You want me to roll you another? I've already done four for you."

"No, no." He struggled to lift two flagons of cider from the back of the truck and groaned with the exertion. Remnants of horse manure stuck to the black and yellow labels having rolled around for the past five minutes. He balanced them on the edge of the truck and cradled them like cherished but grubby twins. He turned his broad shoulders to me and swaggered to the side of the farmhouse using the bottles as ballast.

I followed him to the side door. The warm light drew us like moths to a lamp. He now had the two chubby bottles pinned to his chest with one arm. The other hand was on the doorway steadying himself while he scraped his laceless boots off with the door step. Again, this was an effort. He sighed and nudged the door open with the back of his shoulder.

"Mick. What do you need my supposedly little hands for then?" I kicked his boots off the doormat to one side. I took my riding boots off with greater skill and kicked them to the other side and went into the warm kitchen. I was grateful to get out of the February chill. "I can't be long, mind. It's nearly time to go home."

The smell of woodsmoke filled my nostrils. I saw a loaf of sliced bread and a large tub of margarine on the worktop. Mick was concentrating. He was intent on caring for his newly adopted twins. I don't know if he even heard me. He placed the bottles on the kitchen table and revealed a dark and damp patch on his checked lumberjack style jacket. His face was reddish brown, contrasting with his harebell blue eyes. His mid length hair was unruly - bleached, curled and blow-dried by the elements.

"Do you want me to make sandwiches for the girls ready for tomorrow?" I asked. "What little hands have to do with that though, I don't know."

He gave another sigh and using the table as a launch pad slowly shuffled across the brown lino floor in his thick woollen socks to the old Windsor chair in the corner of the kitchen. He slumped on it. It creaked. At least something did. If it wasn't the chair, it was probably his back. Thirty-odd years of farm labouring was now showing on his tired, puffy, ruggedly handsome face. The cider eased the pain a little.

"Kel, you're a good girl, aren't you."

I tried my best to humour him. "Yes, I'm a good girl. I'm a good girl with little hands apparently."

He gestured me to go over to him. He held his large, shaky hands out to me. The fingerless gloves were old and filthy. I placed my hands on his. He inspected them. "Good. Come on. Jump in the truck. I might need those tonight."

"Where are we going?"

He pushed himself out of the chair and made his way to the door. He slipped into his boots and trudged across the chippings to the front of the farmhouse to the truck. He got in and without any command so did Gyp, the brown and white sheepdog. The self-assured sheepdog's pale brown eyes locked on to mine as if to say in a childish chant, "I-know-where-we're-go-ing!"

The three of us were on our way. To where, I had no idea. We turned out of the trekking centre driveway and continued along the winding lane in second gear. Occasionally we'd risk third gear but mostly stayed in

115

second. The engine was straining and screaming to be released into a higher gear. I had ridden in the lanes many times. I knew the lanes well, but not so well in the dark. It was one of the routes we took pony trekkers. It was strange being in a truck rather than on a horse. The lane seemed narrower and my vision was restricted to ten foot ahead. We were heading further in to the lanes. We passed the point where I would turn the horses around to head home.

"Where are we going?" I asked, again hoping that this time I would at least get a grunt.

"I think you're old enough now to see a bit more of the world. You're clever and sensible. Not like the others. That's why I chose you."

I felt honoured that he had chosen me above the other girls. I think I was high on self-esteem - or was it the clutch fluid and petrol?

We turned into a farmyard. A security light came on. The headlamps of the truck flashed across old farm machinery that was rusting in heaps. They must have been there at least twenty years. There was a white tractor in front of the back door. White with what seemed a reddish brown rash. It seemed to be catching.

Mick turned off the ignition. The truck rolled back and forth for a short while until one of its wheels settled in a small pothole or drain in the yard. A thin sheepdog bolted out of its kennel and barked at us. It didn't get far. It lurched forward on its hind legs as the chain it was attached to became taut like a long metal rod. I opened the door and Gyp leapt over my legs and wandered casually over to the sheepdog with a suave air, his tail over his back. He sniffed the nose of the chained dog and then its behind. Gyp was in love. Again.

"Leave 'em to it," Mick said.

We entered the back door of the farmhouse. A good selection of wellies were strewn around the doorway. I could hear a man's voice inside. A booming voice. We turned into the kitchen and there sat a large man at the end of the table, holding court.

"Well, well, well. Thought you'd forgotten about us. Thought you'd be in the pub, Mick. Who's this then?"

"Kelly's come to give me a hand. Kel, this is Gwilym Morgan."

"I hope you're good at biology, Kelly."

At this point I started to worry. What on earth did they have lined up for me?

"Cup of tea, anyone?"

I felt a sigh of relief as a female voice came from the adjoining room. A large lady entered the kitchen. Her hair was a dark grey wiry mess - like a Brillo pad without the pink bits. She looked as though she took a piece of barbed wire through it every morning to tame it.

"Here's my cup," said the large man.

The woman ignored him. He opened the drawer of the kitchen table and pulled out a small bottle of whisky.

"Oh Good God. I nearly forgot!" shrieked the woman. She bent over to pull one of the oven doors open, her rear eclipsing my view of the large Aga. A cold front washed over the entire kitchen. She stepped aside and produced a lamb. A live lamb from the oven. It looked a little startled but nonetheless alive. I observed with horror.

"Don't worry, bach. It keeps them warm."

And with that everyone started laughing. She disappeared into the other room, made a few chinking noises and returned to the kitchen with willow patterned cups and saucers. She managed to make the tea as well as tending to the semi roasted lamb. I'm sure I could smell cooked lamb through the heady aromas of woodsmoke, greasy wool, whisky and diesel. Steam billowed out of the kettle's spout and I wondered if she was boiling chicks in there. She poured the water into a teapot. I checked closely for yellow fluff. The tea was proudly presented on the table.

Gwilym took one of the cups of tea and poured it into his own cup. It didn't appear to have been washed for some time. He poured a good shot of whisky into the tea. He caught my gaze: "Kills the germs."

I looked at my teacup and convinced myself that it had been hanging on a beloved dresser in the best room and only came out for guests on special occasions. I was confident that not many guests visited Mr. and Mrs. Morgan. I stared at the cup and tried to remember the story of the three fishermen crossing the bridge.

I lost myself in a world of blue and white and began

to make my own stories up while the adults caught up on farming gossip.

"Well, he had it coming, mind, didn't he?" Mrs. Morgan said, shaking her head.

"Aye. That's what Dai Tŷ Draw said anyway…"

Mick looked out of the kitchen window and upwards to the silhouette of a hill. "Right, we'd better make a move. Gwil, how many are up there?"

He poured more whisky into the tea and waved the small bottle in the air "Two or three. One is in the shed." We left the farmhouse. I was intrigued. One what?

We got on the rash-infested tractor. Gyp dumped his four-legged girlfriend and hopped on too. I clung onto the safety frame of the tractor bracing myself against the crisp night air. We climbed the lane up the hill. The tractor was old but didn't falter. We approached a five bar gate.

I hopped off the tractor. The gate was cold as my numb fingers fumbled with the latch. Mick drove through, with co-driver Gyp coolly balanced on board. I climbed back onto the tractor. We bounced along the hard ground, a hundred eyes of assorted sizes stared at us from round grey mounds. Mick stopped the tractor in the doorway of a shed. He left the lights on.

He staggered into the shed and what I could just about make out in the shadows was a pair of shiny sheep eyes. The sweet stench of sheep muck mixed with diesel was overwhelming. The floor was sticky. The sheep bleated slowly and its breathing became heavy and deep.

Mick approached the sheep, saying, "There, there, girl."

"Aw. What's wrong with her?"

"This is where you come in, Little Hands."

"Eh?"

Life Lesson Number One. How to deliver a breech lamb.

When Nothing Helps

Niti Jain

She staggered into the shower. Water cleanses
everything - the dirt, the guilt, the hurt. She scrubbed
hard trying to get it all off.

Stepping back to the room, she realised the shower
didn't help. She tried to sleep - to make her stop
thinking - about being raped yet again - by her
husband. Sleeping didn't help.

Llefain y Lloer

Sian Price

Llyncu llymeidiau o ddŵr oedd ei thasg yn nhawelwch
goleuni gwan y lloer, heb neb yno ond hi a'i meddyliau
a'i phenderfyniadau poenus. Llwyddodd i ddianc o
ddistawrwydd ei hystafell heb ddeffro ei theulu a
chropian yn dawel yn ei gŵn nos wen oedd erbyn hyn
wedi tynhau cryn dipyn o amgylch ei chorff tyner.
Roedd y nosweithiau digwsg wedi talu ffordd; roedd
pob cam wedi ei gynllwynio'n berffaith. Llwyddodd i
sleifio i lawr y grisiau gan osgoi'r ris wichlyd, ond cyn
cyrraedd gwaelod y gris clywodd cwyno cyfarwydd ei
brawd yn ei gwsg, rhewodd a phalu ei hewinedd yn
ddwfn i bren y banister. Arhosodd yno hyd nes iddo
dawelu, heb wybod yn iawn beth oedd achos ei
gwynion ond mi fu hi yno sawl tro yn blentyn yn
gorwedd yn ei gysuro. Ond nid heno, cymerodd yr un
gofal ar y gris olaf a chyrraedd y gegin. Teimlodd ei

Tears of the Moon

Sian Price

In the weak moonlight her task was to gulp water, without anyone there but her thoughts and tiresome decisions. She had successfully escaped the loneliness of her bedroom and had crept away in her white nightgown that had by now tightened around her frail body. Sleepless nights had paved the way; every step had been plotted perfectly, successfully skipping the squeaky stair and eventually reaching the bottom. She froze as she heard the familiar sleeping moan of her brother, and dug her nails deeply into the banister. Never knowing the cause of his moaning, she waited. When they were children, she'd comforted him so many times. But not tonight. She took care creeping to the kitchen. The tiles were cold on her feet and the open fire had long disappeared. Her breath was almost visible. The desire and apprehension choked her

throed yn rhewi ar y teils, roedd y tân agored wedi hen ddiflannu erbyn hyn ac mi oedd hi bron yn siwr iddi fedru gweld ei hanadl. Roedd y pryder a'r awydd i ddianc yn ei thagu ond roedd ei thraed wedi gludio'n gadarn i'r llawr. I hollti tywyllwch y gegin, ystyriodd gynnau cannwyll ond ail-feddyliodd.

Sylwodd ar linyn tenau o olau'r lleuad oedd yn treiddio trwy'r gwydr ac yn goleuo y silff ben tân. Yng nghanol y silff, safai hen ffrâm bren, yn dal llun o'ibrawd a hithau pan yn blant yn eistedd ar wâl garreg y ffarm, hen lun du a gwyn. Wedi bod yn trafod ei dyfodol oeddynt y diwrnod hwnnw ar y wâl, hithau eisiau magu wyth o blant ar y ffarm ac e'n mwydro am ei ddyfodol yn y fyddin, yn cael mynd i saethu "Japs".

Bu bron iddi ddisgyn mewn poen wrth gofio yn ôl ddiniweidrwydd ei phlentyndod, a'i pherthynas pur a'i brawd. Gafaelodd yn dynn yn ei brest oedd yn curo'n gywilyddus wrth iddi edrych i fyw llygaid ei brawd yn y llun; llithrodd ei llaw yn araf i'w bol a theimlo'r panig eto. Mi roedd hi wedi gwastraffu digon o amser; cyrhaeddodd y drws ffrynt a neidiodd i Wellingtons ei thad a thynnu cot neilon ffarm ei brawd amdani. Diolchodd ei bod hi wedi meddwl o flaen llaw ac wedi gadael mymryn o'r drws yn agored i arbed y glep ond wrth iddi ddiolch, teimlodd ei chalon yn suddo wrth iddi gofio ei chelwydd wrth sicrhau i'w thad ychydig oriau yn ôl bod y drws yn bendant ar glo.

Wrth iddi gymeryd ei cham cyntaf, synnodd at dywyllwch y ffarm, ffarm heb groeso oedd hi wedi i'r lleuad ddod ar ei dyletswydd. Sylweddolodd bod

movements and she was glued still. As she fought she noticed a strip of light trickling through the window and shining on the fireplace.

There sitting proudly was a picture of her and her brother as children, sitting on the stone wall, a black and white picture in a wooden frame. They'd been talking about their future that day, her dreaming about raising eight children on the farm and his desire to kill Japs.

She had to fight the urge to scream as she remembered their innocence then and her pure friendship with her brother. To quiet her ache, she clutched her breast as she looked deep into her brother's smiling eyes. She guided her hand slowly to her stomach, and the panic arouse again. She had wasted enough time. She arrived at the front door and jumped swiftly into her father's Wellingtons and pulled her brother's coat around her. She was thankful she had thought ahead and had left the door slightly open earlier, but as she did her heart sunk with guilt, remembering the lie she had told her father that indeed the door was locked.

As she took her first step, she was taken aback by the darkness of the farm. It was a farm with no welcome when the moon came on its shift. The realisation of the trek in front of her hit home and she began to run. After avoiding the death trap that was their yard and awaking the sheep that were sleeping obliviously under a tree, she finally arrived at Cae Bach. It was her favourite field of all the acres of land, good-for-nothing

daith o'i blaen felly penderfynodd mai rhedeg oedd raid. Wedi straffaglu dros y ffald caregog a deffro'r defaid oedd wedi lapio'n gynnes o dan goeden, cyrhaedodd Cae Bach, ei hoff gae o'r aceri o dir oedd ganddynt; hen gae diwerth oedd mae'n wir - y gwair yn felyn hyll, mor ddiflas fel i'r defaid hefyd droi eu trwynau arno ond dyma lle roedd hi a'i brawd bob tro yn cael chwarae yn blant ac yn cael y rhyddid yr oedden nhw'n erfyn amdano. Roedd raid iddi atal y rhedeg am eiliad, gan fod y Wellingtons yn llithro oddi ar ei thraed; teimlodd unigrwydd y cae yn fwy nag erioed a theimlodd y lleuad ym ymwthio'n fusneslyd wrth wylio pob cam.

Clywodd dincian yr afon o dop y cae, roedd hi'n gwybod yn awr nad oedd hi'n bell a chychwynnodd gerdded y tro yma, wedi ymgolli'n llwyr gyda'r sêr oedd yn chwincio arni. Cerddodd yn fyddar i bob dim ac at droed yr afon a'i lygaid wedi hoelio i'r nef. Bu bron iddi ddisgyn ond deffrodd yn sydyn o'i breuddwyd, a throi ei sylw at yr afon ac ar ei hwyneb arnofia'r dail crin yn dawel heb eu tarfu gan yr ymwelydd newydd.

Eisteddodd a theimlo'r oerni a'r glypter yn treiddio'n araf trwy ei gŵn nos. Canolbwyntiodd ar arafu ei hanadl, a thawelu'r peiriant oedd yn curo'n swnllyd yn ei brest. Roedd ei thraed yn ddieithr iddi erbyn hyn yn y Wellingtons gwyrdd a'i bysedd ymhell o fod o unrhyw werth iddi. Tynnodd y got yn dynnach o'i hamglych ac er i'r neilon grafu ei chroen tyner, teimlodd rhyw gysur od wrth arogli'r ffarm a'i brawd. Tynnodd y got yn agosach i'w hwyneb a llenwodd ei a

yellow field that even the sheep turned up their noses at. But this is where she and her brother got to play freely as children. This field allowed the freedom they always craved. The Wellingtons by now were slowly slipping off her feet, so she gave up running. The loneliness of the field crept over her more than ever as she felt the nosy moon watching her every move.

From here, she could hear the trickle of the river. She knew now that she wasn't far; she began to walk again, this time completely lost in the winking stars. Staring into the heavens deafened her. As she slowly approached the mouth of the river, she came to from her dreaming. She dropped to look at the dead leaves swimming freely without noticing the new arrival.

As she sat, she felt the dampness seeping through her nightgown. She focused her concentration on her breathing, quieting the machine that was thumping loudly in her chest. Her feet were strangers to her in the green Wellingtons and her fingers had lost any purpose. She pulled the coat tighter, and even though the nylon scratched her frail skin, she felt a strange pleasure from the scent of the farm and her brother. She pulled the coat to her nose and filled her nostrils with the scent of her brother. In the depth of her thought she felt the months of hiding, heartbreak and longing cascade down her cheeks. She gave in, and let her wounded body fall to the muddy ground, and as she did she let out the scream that had been punishing her for months. This where they were lovers for the first time, laughing, chatting, and kissing. As she thought of her

ffroenau gydag arogl ei brawd; yn sydyn fel rhaeadr yn ei gwddf teimlodd fisoedd o guddio, o dor-calon a gorff clwyfus ar lawr a gadawodd sgrech o boen i hiraethu yn llifo i'w hwyneb. Syrthiodd yn turned up their tails at. atseinio'n rhydd yn y goedwig. Dyma lle y buont yn gariadon amy tro cyntaf, yn chwerthin, yn sgwrsio, yn cusanu.

Wrth iddi feddwl am ei theulu yn cysgu, teimlodd y niwl adnabyddus yn cymeryd ei chorff, y niwl o euogrwydd oedd erbyn hyn yn hen rwtîn. Bu sawl tro lle bu bron iddi gyfaddef, bron iddi sgrechian ar dop ei llais er mwyn i rywun ei hachub o'i boen, ond penderfynu aros yn dawel wnaeth hi bob tro, er mwyn achub eu rhieni o'r cywilydd, ac achub ei brawd. Er roedd pawb yn y tŷ wedi sylweddoli ar y newid sydyn, eu merch bywiog hapus yn sydyn yn gysgod trist, chwerthin am ei phen oedd ei thad gan mynnu mai torri ei chalon dros ei chariad diweddar oedd hi, a'i Mam yn mynnu mai ei hoedran oedd yr achos. Ac eistedd yn dawel wnai ei brawd bob tro. Sychodd y dagrau yn gyflym gan gofio mai nid i grio gyda'r afon oedd ei thasg heno, meddyliodd am y corff cywilyddus oedd yn corddi y tu fewn iddi.

Edrychodd i ddyfnder yr afon a gweld ei hadlewyrchiad anobeithiol yn syllu yn ôl, sylwodd ar ei llygaid du wedi eu chwyddo gan flinder, a'r canhwyllau wedi hen ddiffodd ynddynt, llygaid a fu unwaith yn fflamio gan gariad. Teimlodd yn annifyr wrth glywed ei llais bregus yn cychwyn arllwys ei cyfrinachau i'r afon.

"O dduw, madde i fi! Nid fel hyn oedd hi fod. Fedrai

family asleep, the familiar fog of guilt swept over her. There had been so many times that she had nearly told, confessed, but she had kept quiet every time, saving her family from a lifetime of shame, saving her brother.

Everyone had noticed the sudden change in her, their happy confident girl suddenly a sad shadow, her father made fun of her, blaming some boy from the town.

Her mother blamed her age. Her brother said nothing. She swept the tears from her face and remembered that she hadn't come her to cry; her thoughts faded to the shameful body that was churning inside of her. She looked deep into the river and saw the pitiful reflection staring back at her, her eyes swollen. The candles had faded away, eyes that once flamed with love. She suddenly felt embarrassed as she heard her frail voice pour her secrets into the depths.

"Oh God, forgive me! This isn't how it was supposed to be. I can't, forgive me! I can't have this child, knowing the shame that will come with it. How can I face my family, my brother? I love him, and I know I have no right to love him. I have to put an end to this shame, and end the longing that's in my heart."

As her words echoed, she dug her nails deep into the mud and threw a stone to destroy her reflection. Above her, an owl sang, a hidden stranger to the day, screaming at her not to, but it was too late. She stood there in a confused state; she had not felt these mixed feelings before. Part of her was full of excitement, knowing that the months of hell were finally going to end. She pulled off the coat and Wellingtons and

ddim, madde i fi! Fedrai ddim magu'r plentyn yma, yn gwybod y cywilydd a ddaw. Sut fedrai wynebu fy nheulu, fy mrawd? Rwy'n ei garu, a dwi'n gwybod nad oes hawl gen i ei garu! Mae'n rhaid i mi rhoi terfyn ar y boen, terfyn ar y cywilydd."

Gwasgodd ei hewinedd yn gadarn i'r pridd ar lawr, gafaelodd mewn carreg fechan a'i thaflu'n ffyrnig i ddinistrio'i wyneb yn yr afon.Uwch ei phen roedd y dylluan i'w glywed, yn gyfrinach i'r dydd yn y pellter, ei sgrech bron yn erfyn iddi beidio, ond roedd hi'n rhy hwyr i newid ei meddwl erbyn hyn. Fe fu'n sefyll yno mewn penbleth lwyr am amser; doedd hi erioed wedi teimlo cymysgwch fel hyn o'r blaen, roedd rhan ohoni wedi cynhyrfu'n lân wrth feddwl fod yr wythnosau hunllefus bron â dod i ben. Tynnodd y got a'r Wellingtons a'u gosod yn daclus ar lawr, roedd dyletswydd arni i sicrhau bod y ddau yn cael eu ddychwelyd i'w perchnogion heb eu ddinistrio.

Camodd yn araf i'r afon ac fe deimlodd ei gwn nos yn arnofio'n angylaidd ar dalcen y dŵr. Teimlodd oerni'r afon yn ias ar ei thraed eiddil a'r cerrynt yn drwm. Roedd blynyddoedd o ofni dŵr wedi ei hen anghofio ac mi roedd hi erbyn hyn yn forwyn i'r afon yn cael ei thynnu i'r dyfnderoedd. Wrth iddi gau ei llygaid gwelodd wyneb cariadus ei brawd yn syllu arni, yn gosod y gusan olaf ar ei gwefusau. Teimlodd y treigl tawel, araf yn llenwi ei hysgyfaint a theimlodd y boen yn lleddfu, ar ôl wythnosau o grio a chwyno yn nhawelwch y nos...llonyddwch, yn ngoleuni gwan y lloer.

placed them in a tidy pile on the ground. She had to return these without damage. As she took her first step, her nightgown floated angelically on top of the water. The icy water chilled her delicate feet. Years of fear of the water were forgotten and she was a maiden to the water. As she shut her eyes, she saw the loving face of her brother staring at her, placing the last kiss on her lips. She could feel the cold trickle slowly into her lungs, overwhelming them and she the pain finally began to subside after months of tears and moaning at night...stillness in the weak moonlight.

Ghost in the Garden

Sarada Thompson

It was a bright, full moon night. I like to think moon phases do not affect me, but they always have. This full moon night was no exception. I tossed and turned in bed but I was wide awake. It was around midnight, when I am most alert anyway. However, there was something charged and compelling this night. I had to get up and get dressed quickly. I put on my warm coat, woolly beret and my thermal socks, which I had become accustomed to even in our wet summer months. As I slipped on my boots, I strode out quietly and quickly and paused to admire the garden over the patio. The bed of roses dipped into an almost concealed pond with white water lilies. The gunera had always thrived, and was now an imposing seven to eight feet. It was enchanting to behold - crocosmias in bright, luminous red and orange and the silver birch we had planted to mark our silver anniversary some years ago.

The boundary to our garden was marked by the

clear stream which gurgled past peacefully and only added to the whole atmosphere. It was all so beautiful in the bright fluorescent-lit night. The sky was clear and deep dark bejewelled with bright stars. I was spellbound. An owl screeched, accentuating the still night.

Yet I could not stop for long. I crossed the gravelled yard, and walked over the road for a few feet to our field. And there was Sprite, as if waiting for me.

When we first came to Wales we bought a one-eyed Welsh cob, Vanity, who was in foal. Vanity was going to be sold for horse meat.

When Sprite was born, she was a disappointing light chestnut-coloured foal. Then as she grew, like the proverbial swan, she changed into a beautiful liver-chestnut with almost blond mane and tail. They were my daughter's horses. It was because of the horses we had bought our house with the adjoining land.

My eyes met Sprite's. There was a sort of energy where we understood each other. I got up on the stile near the gate and climbed onto Sprite, who was standing obligingly. As I sat on her, Sprite turned around and walked away. At first she walked, then trotted and then cantered and galloped. It was thrilling to be riding her bare-backed, holding onto her mane, and to feel a refreshing, cool breeze as we gained momentum. As we rode around the field, and slowed down, Vanity stepped out from the deep shadows of the horse chestnut trees. As we walked out together, our two lurcher-sheepdog crosses, Domino and Ringo, came to greet us and run alongside. Not far behind we were joined by our two cats: Marmaduke, our ginger tom-cat, whom we just called 'Catty' affectionately and his 'wife,' tortoiseshell Mumsy. We had a lot of kittens until we finally took Mumsy to the vet.

There we were, the family-menagerie, enjoying the beautiful, moonlit still night.

As we veered around the field, I briefly noticed that none of the pets had shadows. I was more enthralled by the magic of the night and the family around me when I noticed my daughter and son standing by the gate looking in our direction. Sprite took me back to the stile, where I got off. She then joined Vanity near Gayatri. Ringo made a beeline for Ganesh. Domino had already disappeared, being his usual independent self. The cats too had gone, probably hunting.

I approached Gayatri, who was visibly distressed. I put my arm around her. "It is suddenly icy on my shoulder! Mum!" she exclaimed. She shrank away and buried her face into her brother's shoulder and sobbed.

I was hurt and confused. It was me she had always turned to in times of any stress. I became aware as I faltered back that I too did not have a shadow!

It was seven years ago when Mumsy had come over to say goodbye before going back to the barn where she had originally come from. When Domino died, I felt an ache and literal pain right through to my left arm from my heart for a long time.

Then it was fifteen-hand, younger Sprite who rolled over. Surviving nine lives, then it was Catty's turn to bow out.

Vanity had an accident and, after initially pulling

through, succumbed and died on the same day as Ringo the year before.

We had planted horse chestnut trees, dogwoods and cat nips as each left us.

I can only wait with them, as I slowly come to terms as a ghost in the garden.

That Night

Anthony Jones

The flickering fire burned brightly on the beach.
We drank and sang and someone played guitar,
That moonlit night with nothing out of reach
When no one could exhaust our repertoire.

Some spiffs were lit and - God! - we were so drunk
when you and I went walking hand in hand,
investigating all the tidal junk.
I kissed you and we lay down in the sand.

And as the moonlight now lit up your face,
with all our friends now distant and remote,
the beach belonged to both of us - our space! -
I looked into your eyes and now I quote,

"I so adore the lovely bones of you,
Please tell me, Susan, that you love me too."

The End

Niti Jain

And there lies the man I once loved
Shattered, broken, collapsed
On the hard concrete floor
Cold against his skin
Dark in front of the eyes
The pool of blood is the only colour around
It's the only warmth left for him
The hard porcelain coffee mug - broken
The shattered glass of the coffee table around
He lies in the middle of it all
Equally cold as the surroundings
And that is all I have for him in the end
This was to be the end - and it's arrived.

CONTRIBUTORS

Annie Bell-Davies grew up in Ferryside and lives in Carmarthen. Her extensive travels have taken her across the Great Wall of China and through forests in Eastern Europe. She's also made multiple trips to visit her pen-friend of thirty-eight years in Seattle, U.S. A consummate adventurer, Annie's been up in a microlight, swum with dolphins, taken a flying lesson and helped crew a forty foot catamaran. Aromatherapy and rug-making are among her other talents. Her short stories have been published in *Secrets* by DC Thomson.

Rachel Coles was born in Llantrisant, Mid Glamorgan in 1974. One of five sisters, she grew up on a smallholding knee-deep in pondlife, mud, earthworms and other creepy-crawlies. She graduated from Trinity College Carmarthen in 1996 with a BA (Hons) in Theatre, Music and Media through the medium of Welsh. Rachel has always enjoyed writing and was awarded second prize in the Urdd Eisteddfod Scriptwriting Competition in 1992. Her fascination with nature features greatly in her work. She also enjoys flamenco dancing and cooking (not simultaneously of course – now that would be messy!). She currently resides in a small settlement at the near the Cardiff International Airport.

A graduate of Performing Arts, **Martina Davies** has worked for the National Theatre of Wales and in the U.S. She spent time at Rio Grande University, where she was part of a group that wrote and performed drama off-Broadway. She wrote and directed a Welsh language play, *Rhyddid*, which was performed in West Wales in 2009. She has also written and acted in a road safety DVD for the Fire Brigade, which is used in schools as part of a road safety campaign.

Niti Jain was born and bred in New Delhi, India. She believes writing to be her most intimate passion and that is why after receiving a Bachelors in IT, an MBA in Finance and Marketing and working as a journalist and a freelance financial advisor in Delhi, she finally decided to switch fields to take writing seriously. She has learnt various dance forms ranging from Indian Classical, Salsa, Jazz and Belly Dancing! She has also been involved with the theatre circles in Delhi as an actor. She hopes to be a full time writer someday – the day people wouldn't have to worry about earning for survival. Visit her blog: niti-jain.blogspot.com

Hélène James spent her childhood in the UK and abroad. She decided to be a writer at the age of seven following a visit to the local stationery shop where she rearranged their stock of pens and paper. At the same age, her love of dance became clear. However, she followed a different path before developing these loves, opening a Herbal Clinic in 1981 in Swansea and going on to become a Senior Tutor of a Herbal/Homeopathic

College. Since 2007 Hélène has become a teacher of Nia Dance and is now a writer, thereby fulfilling her early dreams.

Anthony Jones was born in Carmarthen, West Wales, in the house where his mother still lives. After leaving Queen Elizabeth Boys' Grammar School, he did a degree at Oxford Poly in Physical Sciences. There he pursued some more creative pursuits, appeared in numerous plays and led a band called *Reg Varney Goes To The Toilet*. He spent most of the eighties in Oxford, either at college or in casual jobs before landing a "proper job" at Nielsen. He returned to Carmarthen where he now lives with his wife Sue, a dog and six cats.

Amanda Miles' ancestry has strong links with Wales. From Milford Haven, she moved to Essex at the age of ten. One of her most enjoyable jobs was in a record store in the 1970's. Amanda trained as a nurse in London and she has a BA (Hons) in Social Science and Administration. Following a major life-changing event, she returned to Pembrokeshire in 2006 where she lives with her husband and their beloved animals. Wales has awakened her personal creativity along with her love of the arts. Amanda has a passion for animals, enjoys Middle Eastern Dancing and is a strict vegan.

Megan Power hails from Nova Scotia. Her work has been published in *America West, San Antonio Express-News, Scene* and *Women's Health and Fitness*. Before moving to Wales she lived and worked in Japan, Mexico, Canada and the U.S. She is currently working on a book of short stories called *Modern Monogamy*. Visit her website: meganpower.blogspot.com

Theatre has always been a major passion of **Sian Price** and she was able to further this through her undergraduate studies in Performing Arts in West Wales. She was fortunate to be able to participate in an exchange programme to America as part of her studies, where she experienced a different culture and enjoyed writing in a new environment. She has worked with some of Wales' best directors and theatre companies, including the National Theatre of Wales. Writing for the theatre has been an interest of hers from an early age. She has recently begun exploring other spheres and genres of writing.

Clare Scott's experience of living in West Africa as a young child has coloured her life. She studied French, German and Italian at university. She has taught foreign languages, English and Drama to children and adults. She has worked as a social worker, developed services and training for sexual health and HIV/AIDS in southern England and West Wales, before changing direction again and becoming a lecturer for specific learning differences at Trinity University College in Carmarthen. She has written for specialist journals and supported developing writers. Now she is concentrating on her own creative writing.

Sarada Thompson is an Indian artist and writer, resident in the UK since 1973 and in Wales from 1990. She was born in Singapore and worked first as a journalist in the Malay Mail/New Nation and the Singapore Herald. When she arrived in London she was set to read law as a member of the Inner Temple, but then spent the next two decades raising a family, writing for the local Northampton Post and the Milton Keynes Weekly during this time. Her work draws on the Hindu classics, the multicultural influences of her background and her life experiences. She has exhibited her art in South Wales and England, led Hindu storytelling workshops and won prizes for her short stories.

Tracey Warr is Lecturer in Contemporary Art Theory at Oxford Brookes University. She has a BA and MPhil in English Literature and a PhD in Art History. She has a substantial list of publications on contemporary art (including *The Artist's Body*, Phaidon, 2000). Her writing has been supported by Arts Council England. She writes children's and adult fiction. She is currently working on a book on art journeys and a historical novel set in 11th century France. Next year she is undertaking a Writer's Residency in a treehouse in the Scottish Highlands, and organising a symposium in Oxford on The Culture of Rowing and Swimming. Visit her website: traceywarr.wordpress.com

ACKNOWLEDGMENTS

The editors and contributors would like to express gratitude to the following supporters.

Thank you to Menna Elfyn, Dr. Paul Wright and Kevin Matherick at Trinity College for their support and encouragement.

Special thanks to Dominic Williams, Marketing Director at Parthian Press, for overseeing this project. This book would not have been possible without his knowledge and advice. Lucy Llewellyn consulted with typsetting.

Thank you to contributor Niti Jain for her work in marketing this book and creating the Shadow Plays website.

MA IN CREATIVE WRITING

TRINITY COLLEGE CARMARTHEN

Trinity's MA in Creative Writing is designed for committed writers who wish to complete significant pieces of work and generally broadened their experience as writers.

The workshop programme is run by one of Wales' leading writers, Menna Elfyn. It draws upon a number of adjunct writing staff, and the support of academics experienced in the teaching of all aspects of creative writing.

In addition to the course itself the University supports a number of reading and social events in which you would be able to participate, as well as the publication of a course anthology showcasing students' work.

Study can either be full-time over one year, or part-time over two.

Coleg y Drindod
CAERFYRDDIN

Trinity College
CARMARTHEN

Experience some of Wales' freshest talent
in this innovative and experimental anthology

PARTHIAN

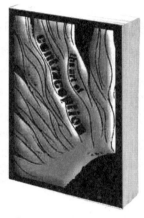

www.BRIGHT YOUNG THINGS.info